FACE-OFF!

Cord meant to have him. Letting Ryker escape was out of the question. This fight was going to be finished. They would divide up the murder charges afterward, over coffee. Ryker, the conniving son of a bitch.

"Ryker!" Cord shouted into the rain.

At the corner of the barn the sawed-off shotgun's muzzle flared....

CORD

Gunsmoke River

Owen Rountree

BALLANTINE BOOKS • NEW YORK

Library of Congress Catalog Card Number: 84-91020

ISBN 0-345-31456-5

Manufactured in the United States of America

First Edition: March 1985

For Dick Hugo
and
For Matt Hansen

Chapter One

"**D**ID YOU EVER WISH WE HAD STAYED IN Montana?" Cord asked abruptly. It was a perfect, bright spring day, made for drowsing in the saddle and drifting with whatever daydreams came to mind, and neither of them had spoken for maybe ten minutes.

"Nope," Chi said. She did not look his way.

"I'm thinking of the timbered mountain country west of the Divide." They were a couple hours north of Trinidad on the broad road to Denver. It ran through immaculate farmlands, models of order and husbandry, the drill rows of spring grain sprouting fragile lines of light green, and all the farmstead buildings freshly painted a brilliant white. Way off to the left, piney forest climbed toward the spine of the Colorado Rockies, the steep ridge line of the Continental Divide draped in snow against a pale clean sky. "Something like this," Cord said.

1

"Montana," Chi repeated. At least she was paying attention.

"You know . . . remember that town on the Clark's Fork of the Columbia . . ."

"New Willard," she interrupted. "Stupid name. We robbed the Equitable Bank, and you ran out on me."

"Hey now." Cord turned in the saddle, but she was smiling, her dark handsome face tranquil in the sunshine's warmth. Her flat-brimmed sombrero hung at the back of her neck from the rawhide thong chin strap, and two thick braids of shining black hair curled out from under it, the ends fastened with elaborate delicate silver clips studded with bits of turquoise. She wore her serape back over her shoulders, and her black leather britches were tucked into the high tops of her hand-tooled boots. Her large-roweled Spanish spurs clicked musically. Fine enough, Cord decided, this pretty day and the woman.

"There was a posse after us, and I had the money," he said. "And you're better on horseback than me, lighter anyway, so I figured you could lead them on a chase while I saw to the goods."

"You've always got a plan. You're the brains of this outfit."

"It worked out, though. You found me."

"*Por supuesto*." Chi laughed. "Lucky me."

"I was talking about Montana," Cord said stiffly.

"Another plan? Tell me a tale, *querido*."

On the far side of a perfectly square field, a young man in coveralls was harrowing newly tilled ground, working a fine dappled gray team. One of the stocky draft animals tossed its head and snorted. The young man waved and Cord waved back. He could not really feature farming as a way of life, but owning a piece of land, that appealed. . . .

"There's country south of New Willard," Cord said,

"down the Bitterroot Valley. It's upriver really, but people say down...it's warmer, that's why, I guess. There's no prettier place for ranching."

"Ranching?" Chi pretended astonishment, as if he had suggested they both enroll in Harvard College to study Romans and Greeks. But she knew where this was heading.

"Well it is. Prettiest place in the West, bar none. Mountains to either side, the Bitterroots and the Sapphires, snowy halfway through summer and creeks coming down every draw so all that bottomland, ten miles wide some places—it's always green."

"Always?" Chi echoed solemnly.

"Right there they got heaven," Cord insisted. "The people who get to live there, own some land."

Chi reined up. "What talk. Do you hear yourself?"

"Sure I do." Cord shook his head. She knew what he was leading to, maybe even wanted to hear it, but she never made it easy for him to say. "I been doing some thinking."

"Yes you have. Never thought I'd hear you put 'pretty' and 'farming' in the same line of talk." She knew about his growing-up days on a hardscrabble quarter-section southeast Texas homestead, how he had fled from that life as soon as he was old enough and able.

"I'm not talking farming." Cord made a sour face. "I'm talking about running cows in fine country, thickest, richest grass you ever saw and water all year, and looking up from whatever to see those mountains. We call that ranching."

"Uh huh"—Chi nodded—"and there's winter. Forty below sorts out the riffraff. Snow all the time and cows to feed every day, and you got to stay and do it."

Cord watched the young farmer turn the team, talking to the grays as he worked the reins. Cord thumped the ribs of his bay gelding and they rode on. "You can hire a man or two who'll work the winter for you, say you have business south. You got land of your own, and cattle. You're a gentleman."

Chi laughed and Cord felt himself color. He was puffing a little hard maybe, but what the hell . . . "People change."

"January in Montana, there's a change all right. I could be in Nogales, sitting in the sun and drinking tequila and listening to folk talk my proper language. You aren't the only one moving on in years." The idea turned her serious. "Maybe I'm getting spoiled. You think I'm spoiled, Cord?"

It was his turn to laugh. She frowned. "Something funny?"

"Maybe we're both getting spoiled. We been running easy these days." That was a good feeling. First off, no law to speak of was seriously interested in their whereabouts. A Federal mix-up about a job they had nothing to do with had been straightened out not long ago, about the same time they'd maneuvered an amnesty out of the venal Governor of Idaho Territory, a fat pig named William Deane Majors. That had cleared the smoke on a Pocatello bank job. Then, just that month, the statute of limitations had run out on the bank job in the town with the stupid name, New Willard. Maybe that's what had started Cord thinking about Montana, and the Bitterroot Valley.

Another thing, for the first time in ten years of partnering, they had a real bankroll, come by honestly, and more legitimate money maybe on the way. A week earlier they'd been visiting their dwarf friend Pell at his mine near New Jerusalem in the San Juan Mountains north of Durango. Pell reported that the shaft would be producing again by July. One third of the profits were Cord and Chi's, for throwing in with Pell in the proud little man's battle against the Denver capitalist who was trying to take over the district. So far the dwarf had delivered $10,000 into their account in the National Bank of Tucson, and most of it was still there, awaiting possibilities.

"Two *viejos*," Chi said. "Settled down on a pretty plot of land with our cows and our hired man, like rich folk. Is that about right?"

"See there." Cord pointed up the trail.

"Qué?"

"There's Montana, about seven hundred and fifty miles that way. Well hell, we're already heading in the right direction."

Chi began to laugh again, shaking her head and clutching at her gut, and Cord started laughing too, couldn't stop himself. Chi reached over and touched a warm hand to his knee, and they went on laughing. There was not a thing wrong, and there was the joke.

"We'll take a look," Cord announced.

"Si, como no?" Chi answered gaily.

Nearby, a woman screamed.

It was a shrill ugly noise, full of hurt. The shriek cut off for a moment then began again, coming at Cord as out of a dark place in a bad dream.

"There." Chi pointed, then spurred her horse. The road here ran along a bench above a glacial swale where a stream swollen with runoff ran muddy amid willows. Up ahead the main road swung right with the bench while a wagon trace turned down toward the creek. The woman's scream came from there. Cord raced after Chi.

From the lip of the bench's cutbank the wagon track switchbacked down to some small rancher's fenced-off creek-edge grassland, triple-strand barbed wire enclosing fifty or so head of white-faced Herefords, new calves nuzzling the paps of the cows. Across the meadow, the corner of a small neat frame house peeked out from the willows along the water. The track passed through a rail gate, and a Wells, Fargo Concord coach was parked nearby.

The rest was old news, and not pretty.

Up on the box a man was folded over a shotgun, his head between his knees and his canvas pants greasy with blood. The driver stood off to the side near the coach's open door, dusty and looking more annoyed than frightened. Beside him stood a heavy, sweating man in a dark suit and high celluloid collar, his vest taut as a drumhead across his belly. His angular hatchet-faced wife, swathed from ankle to chin in a severe black dress, trembled like a dry leaf. The third passenger was a young redheaded sport in a straw boater, checkered jacket, and bow tie. All of them stared straight ahead at nothing, as if at the funeral of someone they did not know well.

One road agent sat horseback at the head of the team of four, holding the animals in check. He had a rifle tucked under his arm. Another covered the passengers and driver with a sawed-off Remington shotgun.

The third bandit was down off his horse near the gate, past the front of the coach where they could all see. He was wrestling with a blond woman in her early twenties. She could have been pretty if her features were not contorted with fear. She screamed and tried to strike the outlaw and hold down the skirts of her yellow dress and voluminous petticoats at the same time. The outlaw slapped at her ineffectually.

The other two were darting quick glances, waiting their turns with the girl. The fat capitalist and his wife went on gazing stonily ahead, but the young man was poised forward with his weight on the balls of his feet, anticipating the chance to do something. At the fence's gate, the road agent had the blond woman turn around and was trying to bend her over the top rail. The woman back-kicked him in the shin, and he grunted a curse.

Cord's first reaction was instinctive: He did nothing. A decade on the outlaw trail had imparted the habit of noninvolvement in this sort of business. There was never any reward except trouble.

Chi drew her Winchester from its saddle scabbard and dismounted in one fluid motion. She levered a .44 cartridge into the breech, lay out full-length on the edge of the bench, and fired, just that quick, without contemplation or hesitation. With a lifetime of these moments behind her, she moved as unconsciously as a dancer. She shot the attacking road agent high in the back. His spine shattered and he spun around and flopped against the terrified woman. She pushed him away in a blind panic. There was blood on her hands and on the front of the yellow dress.

The rifleman at the head of the coach team swung around and looked for a target. Chi shot him out of the saddle. His neck snapped when he hit the ground, and the man with the shotgun was looking around in confusion. The redheaded kid climbed up his back, jerked the sawed-off double-barrel up hard against the man's Adam's apple, and rode him facedown into the grass. The man tried to gasp and passed out.

The team of horses pranced sideways with a great rattling of harness chains. The driver jumped to the head and put his weight on their bridles.

Chi was back in the saddle and spurring her mare into a hard dangerous plunge over the edge to the wagon track. Cord followed more carefully, feeling less than committed to all of this.

The blond woman looked at the blood on her hands and screamed once more. She scrambled up over the fence rails and half fell on the other side. Her dress ripped. She got to her feet and ran, aimless and hysterical.

Chi raked the mare with the big rowels. The horse gathered its haunches and flew over the gate, Chi high and forward in the saddle. Cows looked up stupidly and trotted out of the way.

Cord drew up beside the stage. The kid in the boater was standing over the shotgunner, covering him with his own double-barrel. The man's nose was broken but he was alive and making bubbly sounds. The fat capitalist and his bony wife were huddled together, looking primarily outraged now that the danger was past. "See to the guard on the box." He was a man used to ordering others to do the unpleasant jobs, and having those orders followed.

"Dead," Cord said.

"You must make certain."

"*You* make certain," Cord snapped. "I've seen enough to know." He had no longing to crawl up there on that box with the stiffening remains of somebody gone from the earth.

"Don't take that tone of voice with me, my man."

"I'm not your man," Cord said savagely. You are riding along on a fine spring day and seconds later there is blood everywhere. "I'm starting to get ragged, mister, and when that happens I get crazy. You don't want to mess with that— no telling what might happen."

The sport in the boater barked an abrupt laugh. Cord kept looking at the fat man. "Excuse yourself." This sort of bullying was pointless, and Cord wished he hadn't started it. But dammit, Chi had killed two men, with good reason probably, but still . . . Killing didn't sit well with him on such a day or any day.

"I . . . I beg your pardon, sir." Even stammering, the businessman sounded haughty.

The jaunty kid in the boater was watching Cord curiously. Cord looked away, toward the snowy mountains. He wished trouble on no one these days, but these people did not belong out here. They should have stayed in their city, huddled together against rough play such as this.

The blond woman made the edge of the swollen creek before Chi caught her. She was into the water and Chi plunged after, the mare's hooves throwing up clots of mud.

The woman sunk to her knees in the brown water. Chi climbed down, dropped the mare's reins. The blond hid her face with her hands and began to sob, and Chi stood for several moments staring down at her. Then Chi pulled her to her feet and said some soft thing in her ear. The woman looked at her and nodded. Chi walked her up on the bank, her arm around the woman's shoulder. Chi sat beside her on the grass, rocking and crooning.

"Inevitable." The hatchet-faced woman had a voice like a saw cutting metal. "An unattached woman has no business on the highway."

Cord pointed the finger of his gun hand at her. "Keep your bad news to yourself, lady." Her mouth flew open like a window shade and she turned to her husband, but he'd retired from this fray.

"She said she was a seamstress." The redheaded kid spoke absently, as if he were thinking of something else as he looked up at Cord. "Came here from Elmira, New York, three months back, but she couldn't find a situation and neither could her husband, except up at the mines around Cripple Creek. A week ago him and six other waddies were killed in a cave-in, she told me. She's on her way to Denver to stay with his second cousin. Some fine beginning in our West, don't you think? Say, I know you."

"How's that?" The quick turn took Cord by surprise.

"Sure I do," the young man said. "You are Mr. Cord, the gunman, and that woman yonder is Miss Chi." He turned. "Hold the firestick, friend." He tossed the shotgun under-handed to the startled fat man. The weapon terrified him, as if it were a live snake. The fat man scrambled three steps backward and nearly fell. The gun hit the ground and for some reason did not discharge.

The young man took a small pad and a pencil from the inside pocket of his checkered jacket. He wet the tip of the pencil on his tongue and smiled at Cord in a professional way, like a dentist holding pliers behind his back. "What brings you and your partner to Colorado, Mr. Cord?"

"Who the hell are you, boy?"

"Sorry." He dug into his jacket pocket again and came out with a business card. "Pete Stark, *Rocky Mountain News.* I been down at the Springs, covering the dedication of the city hall. Hot item. But damn, look at the story I got now."

"What story?"

"Yours. A fancy-handed gunslinger riding our local trails."

"You keep me out of your stories." But Cord had the unpleasant feeling his bluster wouldn't work so well with the kid. Too cocky. Maybe if he put a bullet about four inches above the boater . . .

"Can't," Pete Stark said airily. "You're news, Mr. Cord."

Chi was leading her horse toward them, her arm around the shoulders of the girl. Chi removed the rails in the gate and then replaced them after maneuvering the girl through. The girl stared at the body of the man who had touched her, until Chi turned her head away. The girl was wet and muddy. Her face was chalk-white and her hair tangled, and she was trembling. She looked driven from any notion that the world might make sense, and why not? A widow one day, and now splattered with a dead man's blood.

Chi was trembling too, with rage. Cord watched her help the woman inside the stage. The others were also staring: There was something mesmeric about the young widow, weeping and ruined, and the gunwoman Chi, so willing to kill.

Chi came out of the stage. "See to her," she ordered the hatchet-faced woman. The woman covered her mouth with the back of her hand, then did as she was told.

"Where are you heading, Miss Chi?" It was Stark, the reporter.

Chi looked at him as if he were a verminous insect. "Who is the *cabrón* with the big mouth?" she asked, speaking to Cord.

Cord shook his head. She was charged with rage, and Stark was too blithe to see how deeply he was digging his own hole. To head her off from pointlessly abusing him might require some confrontation with her on Cord's part, which he did not relish. But then, at Chi's feet, the surviving road agent stirred and lifted his shaggy head. He was unshaven. His mouth opened and closed; he didn't seem to have teeth, but his gums were white as bone.

Chi kicked him in the ear. The outlaw stiffened like a sledgehammered steer, shuddered, and drew into a little convulsion before lying still again. Cord wondered if he was dead. The businessman gasped and even Stark looked concerned.

Chi looked up at Cord: *Here we are again, the same old trouble you never asked for, dogging you wherever you go.* Cord had no argument with that, but there was no longer any simple riding away from this one, especially not with Chi in this dangerous frame of mind.

Staring awful fire at them all, Chi stalked to her mare, threw up a stirrup, and began to check the cinch. "Get in," the driver said to the businessman and the reporter, not pleasantly. The only response came from within the coach, the blonde's whimpering and the awkward ineffectual murmurings of the older woman, ancient sounds echoing human frailty. Cord stared at Chi's back, dreading the sense of misadventure possessing him.

Chapter Two

THE BROWN PALACE HOTEL OOZED LUXURY. The lobby was all potted plants, Doric columns, and leather-upholstered divans stuffed fat as babies' cheeks. The rug had strange Chinese-looking characters worked into the border, and traversing it was like walking through dewy grass. The desk clerk was old enough to have seen some things and cautious enough to refrain from commenting on the dust on a man's boots, or the way he happened to wear his gun.

Cord was established in a two-room corner suite on the fifth floor. The bedroom was larger than the cabin in which Cord had been reared. Its centerpiece was a double-size bed, with crackling stiff sheets, huge plump pillows, and a quilted coverlet that might have cost someone's grandmother months of close work. There were gleaming brass spittoons on either side of the bed; you never could tell who would need to spit, or when.

The sitting room had lace-framed windows on two sides, brocaded armchairs, red velvet wallpaper, oak tables a rich man would not spurn, and another deep Oriental carpet, brought over on sailing ships from the markets of China. There was a fireplace with a painting of a rosy plump woman above the oak mantel, and opposite, a full-length mirror of fine beveled crystal.

Cord examined himself in its clean gleaming perfection. Some fine outlaw, he thought, wallowing in elegance like a hog in mud. But Cord had to smile, and his reflection smiled back: he would make a fine millionaire. Take about five minutes to get used to this sort of thing.

For years Cord had felt crowded and half suffocated when sleeping inside, and would wake up gasping from dreams about falling from great heights into bottomless icy water. There was still nothing finer than sleeping under a sky bright with summer stars arranged in their orderly constellations by nature's artful hand. On the other hand, this Brown Palace Hotel wasn't bad for the odd night. Cord raised an eyebrow at his reflection, like a French farceur flirting with the crowd.

Maybe Pell's mine would strike big and they really would be rich, have all the money there ever was—what then? Would Chi stick with him, or maybe bring her money home to some dying village deep in Mexico? Cord shook his head at himself. Old habits, like never counting on what a person might do, died hard. Chi seemed happy enough to be with him these days, even willing to take a look at that Bitterroot country in Montana, knowing he was toying with notions of settling in, knowing he might ask her to kick in a few thousand toward the land and the cattle. . . .

Cord stood at a window and looked down at the corner of 17th Avenue and Tremont Place. The cobblestone streets were clogged with fancy four-horse teams drawing lurching buckboards and trams, the drays of dairymen and butchers and greengrocers making their daily deliveries. Men in somber suits marched briskly along the raised sidewalks to meetings and all sorts of important dealings; women in velvet hats and veils carried woven straw shopping baskets in the crook of the arm as they stared through plate-glass shop windows. The stores in this part of downtown were mostly expensive, vending luxuries that few Westerners would ever have, or miss: a millinery, haberdasher, barber salon, a cocktail bar with discreetly tinted windows where a banker could take a bracer without upsetting any skittish depositors. Panhandlers moved against the current of pedestrians with palms outstretched; street merchants sold hot chestnuts, Frankfurt sausages, neckties. At the corner, a slick-haired sharper ran a monte game on a folding stand, while loafers leaned against the stone buildings with one leg up, chewing at match sticks and soaking up the spring sunshine.

Cord gazed across the street and up at the six- and seven- and eight-story granite-faced neo-Gothic facades. He was looking at the advancing frontier of a new way of living in the West, and did not hate it so much as he might have. Still, it reminded him that if he wanted to reserve an unpaved piece of the country, he'd best get on with it. There were still ways to have it all—live mostly in the country but once in a while, a couple weeks of the year, succumb to a taste of life in Seattle or San Francisco, maybe winter a month or so in Arizona or the northern fringes of Old Mexico. Take the train, spare yourself those long, rump-busting days in the saddle. . . .

Chi rapped sharply on the door and let herself in. She did not look to be in any mood to discuss settling down or any other romantic foolishness. "Look here," she ordered, and shoved a copy of that day's *Rocky Mountain News* at

Cord. The story was in the left-hand column of the front
page.

YESTERDAY'S OUTRAGE

Road Agents' Depredations on
the Colorado Springs Stage

NOTORIOUS DESPERADOS TURN SAVIORS

The Day Is Saved by
the Most Unlikely Hand

by J. Pete Stark
Correspondent

April 27, *en route* to Denver—Not
since the days preceding Statehood, and
not often then, has the Denver to Colorado Springs Post Road witnessed such
spoliation, nor absorbed into its ruts such
quantities of life's crimson ichor, as occurred this day at the 24th milepost, just
off the turnpike near the ranch of Karl
Baumgartner.

With uncanny prescience, this correspondent was attached to the party on
the Wells, Fargo coach which was set
upon by three road agents a few minutes
before the hour of two, post meridiem,
this day. Indeed, we were not only witness but willing combatant in the revolt
that overthrew the bandits, and our account is therefore unimpeachable.

Cord skimmed several paragraphs about how the stage
was ambushed, the driver forced to pull off the highway,
the passengers off-loaded and robbed of their pocketbooks
and watches. Stark had a fine time writing about the valiant
death of the shotgun guard when he tried to get the drop,

and hit a real lick with the part about the "unwanted attentions" paid to the young widow, whose name was Rachel
Wright.

"I am going to pay that newspaper boy some 'unwanted
attentions,'" Chi said darkly. She had come from visiting
with the Wright woman.

"How is she?"

"How would she be?" Chi snapped. She looked out the
window, her back to him. "I can't stand that kind of business. It makes me want to kill. Shooting scum like those
men is natural as scraping manure off your boots."

"All right."

"She's starting to come back to herself, and learned
something about being tough. She'll have to stay tough all
her life."

"Like you," Cord chanced.

She turned and her expression finally relaxed. "I can't
help staying tough. Like a horsemeat steak."

Cord continued reading. Stark's prose grew more breath-
less when he got to the sudden appearance of Cord and Chi.

> At once the first ruffian's head sep-
> arated entirely from his shoulders and
> his pestilent hands fell away from the
> woman. In the blink of an eye the sec-
> ond ruffian clutched at his chest and
> tumbled from his mount. We saw to the
> third ruffian ourself, bolding removing
> his shotgun and thrashing the coward
> with his own weapon.
>
> Imagine our astonishment when we
> looked fully upon the visages of our
> providential saviors and beheld faces we
> had seen previously—upon the Court-
> house wall, lithographed on wanted

posters. We beheld the notorious Cord
and Chi.

   Could they have reformed? we wondered. They had been our deliverance,
so it was with no little relief that we
learned from Mr. Cord that he and his
"sidekick" were, by virtue of amnesty
or time's forgiveness, no longer fugitive
from either the Federal Government or
the several States and Territories.

Chi was reading over his shoulder. She stabbed at the
last paragraph with a forefinger. "What's this? I didn't read
this part before, was afraid this Stark's writing was curdling
my breakfast in my gut."

"'Neither of our rescuers knew that the Wells, Fargo
company had posted with officials of Denver County a $2,000
reward for the capture or carcass of each of the road agents,'"
Cord read aloud. "'It was our pleasure to so inform them.
Mr. Cord, whose manner is surpassingly polite and gentle,
demurred. "The satisfaction of aiding the legal order and
helping justice prevail," he told us, "is reward enough."'"

"What the hell?" Chi demanded. "You turned down six
thousand dollars without saying anything to me?"

Cord folded the newspaper and slapped it against his
thigh. "In a way of speaking. It didn't seem like something
we wanted to get mixed into."

Chi stalked to the door. "We're going to turn the money
over to the woman—she needs it more than Wells, Fargo.
I'm going to send that newspaper boy a message."

"I already did." Cord looked sheepish. "I changed my
mind."

She stared at him. Cord cleared his throat, knowing she
would hate the next part. "The sheriff is coming around
tomorrow morning with a bank draft. We can change it to

currency right after, be out of town and halfway to Wyoming by sunset." He avoided meeting her scowl. "One more day. I'll take care of it. You don't have to deal with the sheriff or any bankers."

"When do we give the money to the Wright woman?"

"*We* don't. My three thousand is going to buy land in the Bitterroot Valley."

"Blood money," Chi spat.

"Just money."

"You say so."

"Those boys were trash, should have been shot a long time ago. They were giving the profession a bad name." It was halfway a joke, but true just the same. "It's legal money," Cord insisted, "ours free and clear."

"You think what it will buy," Chi pressed. *Not me—it won't buy me.* She opened the door and stopped with her back to him. "Rachel Wright can get by with three thousand," she said. "That's more than anyone ever gave me."

She turned and stabbed a finger at him. "Just try not to act too much the fool when you take that money, *querido*. I don't like to see your name attached to foolishness. Makes me look foolish too, for partnering with you."

She waggled the finger. Cord gaped at her and muttered, "Do my best," but by then she was on her way.

Chapter Three

CORD KEPT A CAREFUL EYE ON THE PEOPLE jostling past on the sidewalk along California Street, and one hand over the bulge in his vest where the $6,000 in new banknotes rode. Here was something new: afoot in the middle of a metropolis and worried about some petty pickpocket getting lucky.

In Cord's other hand was a bright bouquet of spring flowers. The old woman holding down the street corner, surrounded by baskets full of great sprays of yellow and golden and purple blossoms, had smiled at Cord when he handed over his four bits. "Going to call on your sweetie?" She smirked. "She sees you coming with them flowers, she'll pull the drapes and be first up the stairs." The woman's breasts rested on her flaccid belly. She winked hugely. "I would, anyway."

Cord could stand that too; he'd been feeling the fool most of the morning. The day's business began in the editorial chambers of the *Rocky Mountain News*, where blue tobacco smoke drifted near the ceiling. The sheriff of Denver was a thick man with a huge star of real gold and a hearty handshake, probably quite a popular fellow with the ladies and the voters and the boys at his drinking club. He was, anyway, politic enough not to bring up Cord's early history when he handed over the money. Pete Stark grinned at the ceremony over his Remington typewriter, while a quick-sketch artist flashed charcoal over a pad, fashioning a likeness of the scene for the late edition.

Cord took the check, told Pete Stark that he was about as interested in cooperating on a series of articles about his life as he was in being gelded, and got the hell out of there. He left the sheriff standing with his right hand proffered, looking like a bride abandoned at the altar.

At the First Bank of Colorado, Cord stood on line behind a woman wearing a straw hat with a wire-and-crepe-paper flower sticking out of the crown. On one cocked hip she balanced a fat little boy. The kid stared over his mother's shoulder at Cord. Cord disliked children, because he never knew how to react to them. He wished the woman would wipe the brat's nose so decent citizens were not disgusted.

But the bank teller was pretty as ever a working girl would be, her silvery blond hair shiny clean and halfway down her back in a daring fall. Cord gave her the bank draft and a smile. "Bet you're from Dakota."

The girl held the draft by the corner with two fingers. She examined it, then Cord, with the same fish-eyed distaste. "Why?" she said finally.

"Because you look like the handsome daughter of some north-country Swede."

She gave him a narrow glance, as if he had spoken in Hebrew. "Why does someone of your sort have this much money?"

"Good luck, I guess." Turning up the smile won him nothing.

The teller showed him the look reserved for her most trying situations. "A bank draft for six thousand dollars is not a matter for levity," she announced witheringly.

Cord flexed his jaw, as if trying to find the right words behind his wisdom teeth. "No reason to cry, either. That's drawn against the County of Denver."

"For what?"

Cord was running shy of patience. His experience with banks ran mostly to unauthorized withdrawals, but he knew when his reins were being jerked. "See here," he said, beginning a speech about the rights of common citizens.

"Do you have any identification?" the girl interrupted.

Cord's mouth dropped open. He looked around, as if he might find an ally close by. The snot-nosed kid, waiting for his mother at the writing desk, extended his right hand, thumb and forefinger out stiff, the other three folded into a fist. The kid waggled the thumb and said, "Bang. You're dead, Mister."

On the wall above the kid, a sheaf of papers was pinned to a cork board. Cord riffled through them, found what he wanted near the bottom. He ripped the poster down and slapped it in front of the teller. "That's me," he said. It was year-old Federal paper offering $5,000. The line drawing wasn't a bad likeness, actually.

"You will have to speak with the president," the teller said to the poster, and disappeared through a door at the end of the counter. She came back thirty seconds later and said, "Step aside, please."

Cord lounged against the counter beside her cage while she served other people. Maybe five minutes passed. "Are you?" Cord asked.

The girl blinked eyes blue as a frozen tarn. "What?"

"The daughter of a Swede from Dakota?"

She thought about that. "I am a woman who works for every dime she sees."

Cord smiled hugely. "We could make a deal along those lines."

Her icy blue eyes widened and her mouth clamped shut. A uniformed bank guard came up, cleared his throat, and said his name, and Cord was saved.

He followed the guard through a gate at the end of the railing and into the office of a smiling handsome man in a pinstriped suit. He was about Cord's age, too young by Cord's stereotype of a bank president. They shook hands. Cord's $6,000, in hundred-dollar notes, was stacked neatly on the banker's desk.

"I understand you have faced flying lead many times, Mr. Cord," the banker said cordially. "How did that compare to facing our Miss Winter?"

Cord opened and closed his mouth.

"Three days ago," the banker said, "Miss Winter's fiance ran away with a cocktail waitress from the Buckhorn Casino. The experience sharpened an already finely honed disposition."

"I got away without being cut," Cord said. "Born lucky." The young banker laughed with genuine humor.

The banker had packed the cash into an envelope for Cord, and now as he entered the lobby of the Brown Palace with his fistful of flowers, Cord touched at it again. The clerk was right about one thing. Six thousand dollars was no joke.

Look what you've become, Cord thought. *A goddamned goat for money!* He had to smile at himself, and he nodded jauntily to the desk clerk and went up the stairs two at a time. He knocked on Chi's door, and she called, *"Ven."* Cord turned the knob, took the envelope of money from his vest pocket, and pushed the door open with the toe of his boot.

Chi was not alone. Cord felt foolish once again, and this time, angry at himself as well: coming through a door with both hands full was the sort of stupid error that could cost you a fraction of a second of speed, and your life.

A bony little man sat with his pigeon rump perched on the edge of one of the brocaded armchairs in Chi's parlor. He leapt to his feet and advanced on Cord. He didn't seem to realize that Cord's mitts were occupied until he stuck out his own right hand. Cord stared at him. The little man wiped his hand on the front of his coat. "You're Cord, right?"

Cord nudged the door. He regarded the man, who took another tentative bird-step and stood worrying with nervous fingers at a derby hat.

"Who asks?" Cord glanced at Chi and got no help. She was leaning back against the red, velvet-covered wall, her arms somewhere under her serape.

"The name is Pearl. Bernard Pearl." He automatically offered his hand again and immediately pulled it back, as if afraid Cord might give him the flowers. He clenched and unclenched his fingers.

"Here," Cord said, in what amounted to an angry tone. He shoved the flowers at Chi. She stared for a long moment, then accepted the bouquet without meeting Cord's eyes. She might have been fighting laughter, or preparing to whip the blossoms alongside his head.

Bernard Pearl stood maybe four inches above five feet and looked like he would dress out around a hundred pounds. He was anemically thin, as if his bones were fine as a robin's. He was dressed like a comic character in one of Dickens's newspaper serials. His stovepipe trousers ended three inches above knobby ankles encased in sagging gray-white hose and low-cut shoes with laces knotted in several places where they had broken. His vest was tight enough to outline ribs, and the sleeves of his waistcoat were too short and drew attention to his long-fingered womanish hands. Under the coat he wore a wrinkled cardboard shirt-front, a high stiff celluloid collar, and a bow tie so red it reflected pale color onto his hollow pocked cheeks. His black hair was parted in the middle and slicked down with greasy pomade, hard and flat as patent leather. The clothing needed a brushing, and there was a soup stain on the shirt-front.

"What is this?" Cord asked Chi. She shrugged. She had her nose down closer to the flowers, like she might be sniffing them.

"I hear you folks are riding north."

Cord looked at Pearl. "Where did you hear that?"

Pearl smiled. His teeth were etched with black rot. "I read that story in the *News*, about how you did them road agents, saved that girl from a fate worse than death, like the man says. Story said you were leaving town soon as you collected your due. I thought maybe you're heading for Wyoming."

"He talked at me for five minutes," Chi said into the flowers. "Never said anything I could make sense of." She held them in both hands against her breast.

Pearl squared his shoulders resolutely, as if contemplating a naked jump into a snowdrift. "Listen here. I got to get to Casper, see. You came in from the south, and you ain't heading west over the mountains, not this early in the season, so you are going to either Kansas or Wyoming. Well nobody would go to Kansas, not unless his mother dropped him on the head when he was a baby." Pearl gave Cord a manly, conspiratorial wink. Cord scowled and Pearl lost a measure of self-assurance. "So maybe not. No hard feelings, right?" Pearl put his derby hat on his head, tapped the crown in a careless dapper way, and headed for the doorway.

Cord took his arm and Pearl jumped about a foot in the air. "Don't get your back hair up." Cord laughed. "Not that you could, with all that goose grease." Close up Cord could smell the little man's foul breath, flavored with a whiff of stale beer. "You drunk or crazy?" Cord asked.

"I don't wish to travel alone," Pearl said stiffly. "I have sufficient reason. I'm carrying valuables, what you might call *goods*." Pearl gave Cord another insincerely fraternal smile. "I hate the idea of taking chances."

Chi turned away from the window. "What did you steal, *Señor Perla*?"

"How's that?" Pearl drew himself up. "Oh I get it, a joke. Haw haw."

Pearl reached inside his too-small waistcoat. Cord stiffened and put his hand on the butt of his Colt .45 Peacemaker. Strangers' hidden hands were once in a while the prelude to terrible trouble. But Pearl came out with an untidy wad of greenbacks. He began smoothing the wrinkled bills, turning them right side up, wetting a greasy thumb and counting. "One hundred, two hundred, three . . ." He looked up when he got to $1,000 and waved the money at Chi. "You two are riding through Casper, or at least it's not so far out of your way, that's how I figure it. You let me ride along, I pay you a grand. You couldn't make easier money if you printed it yourself."

"All of a sudden everyone wants to give us money," Chi said. *"Por nada."*

"That's right." Pearl smiled like a missionary whose preaching had suddenly reached some dusky heathen. "Nothing at all."

"Say someone catches up, though," Cord said. "Say they

are willing to use guns to get at what you're carrying. You look at it that way, a thousand dollars is cheap protection."

"It ain't that way. This is legal." He tried a rat-faced grin. "Besides, I hear you two don't have much compunctions about shooting, or the law."

"You didn't hear the rest, *Perla*," Chi said. "About how we don't need your money, or how maybe we'll just take it away from you, right now. All your chatter, and you left out the best parts."

"First off, what are you carrying?" Cord asked.

Pearl shook his head and started a smart answer, but Cord cut him off. "You tell me. If we are even going to consider doing business, you speak — speak straight — when you're spoken to."

"Don't be that way." This time Pearl moved more gingerly when he reached into his coat; he hadn't missed Cord's gun hand move. He extracted a clean sheaf of papers and unfolded it to show Cord the top sheet. It had an ornate calligraphic title and an official-looking seal. "I'm a confidential agent," Pearl said confidentially. "I look into things."

"You ought to look into a new wardrobe," Chi said.

"You got a nasty mouth, lady."

There was a beat of silence. "Yeah," Chi said. "I also got a mean streak about a mile wide, right at the moment. You want to say another thing, see what happens?"

Chi put down her flowers on the oak sideboard and took two steps toward the little man. Pearl stood transfixed.

"You want those filthy rotten teeth knocked down your throat?" Chi was slipping into the darkest hole in her nature.

Cord said, "Chi!"

She looked at him blankly for a moment. Still watching her, Cord said out of the side of his mouth, "Tell the rest. Make it clean and fast."

Pearl came back to himself. He refolded the legal papers. "I'm working for a lawyer in Casper, fellow named Meeker. You probably heard of him."

"I don't hear from lawyers much."

"Maybe not." Pearl risked a quick sideways look at Chi. "Anyway, this Meeker has a client, name of Cecil Beasman, and this Beasman has considerable ranching interests— maybe a couple of hundred thousand acres and half of it deeded, up on the Belle Fourche. So here it comes spring and Beasman is ready to turn out his cows—or have his people do it, since Beasman doesn't much fancy quitting the Cheyenne Club in favor of the range these days—and some company of nesters files a legal suit, challenging Beasman's rights to maybe six miles of river front bottomland."

Pearl shook his papers in Cord's direction. "A week back, Meeker sends me down here on the train to see what I could dig up, which was plenty. I got these at the state archives going all the way back to Territorial days and covering land from here to California, Canada, Mexico, and the Mississippi. Old titles still good as gold, and soon as the Federal judge in Casper sees them the nesters are going to be standing outside their own bob-wire fences, surrounded by their furniture and wondering what happened."

"Maybe the law is on the side of them nesters."

"Haw, haw. You reading me the law, Mr. Cord?"

"Finish up," Cord snapped. Maybe it *was* funny, coming from someone who had run outside the law for so long, but he'd never stolen from a sodbuster nor anyone else except the bankers, whom he'd considered something of a thief like him. He'd sure as hell never let some big-city moneyman take *his* land away.

"I'll play along," Pearl said. "The bottomland belongs to the nesters. Okay. But whether or not you ride me up to Casper, they are out on their asses. Now then..." Pearl replaced the papers under his coat. "You want a thousand dollars or not? Like you figure, this Beasman has plenty of green cabbage, and a thousand less ain't going to cramp his style. Every day them nesters insist on acting stubborn costs him lots more, plus some pride. So Lawyer Meeker wants these papers pronto, and I am authorized to pay you this money, which I picked up at Western Union this morning, after I read the fine press that kid Stark gave you."

Pearl was blathering along with too much confidence for Cord's taste. "You came down on the train. Go back the same way."

"That'd be swell with me. I never have got on with horses. But there is no train, not for two weeks at least. There's extra snow in the mountains this year, and three trestle bridges washed out in the runoff in the week since I came down. Seems like fate to me. How about you?" Pearl grinned.

The story was okay, the money easily made. Cord looked toward Chi, but she had picked up the flowers and was holding her silence at the window with her back to him.

"Step outside," Cord told Pearl. "Wait in the hall. Bide your time."

When the door closed behind Pearl, Cord said, "It sounds like found money to me."

"You've got money on the brain," Chi said. "Give you a sniff at property, you go for it like a goat to pansies."

"Where did you hear that? That sounds like stage comedy."

"Might be," Chi said. "I heard it from you." She laughed and lowered her head to sniff the flowers. "Here's something funny—so far, the last three days stink worse than Pearl."

Cord looked at her, utterly bewildered. Chi laughed again. Cord watched her put the flowers in the pewter water pitcher that sat on the oak sideboard. "All right," he said weakly.

"Five days from now we ditch him in Casper. Couple of weeks after that we are in Montana with an extra five hundred each. Okay?"

"Bueno. We'll buy another thousand dollars worth of land." She brushed a hand over the bouquet in the pitcher. "And raise flowers."

"You listen . . ."

Chi shook her head ruefully. "Bring in *Señor Perla,*" she said. "We got to get moving. Some other hombre is looking at our little rancho right this minute."

Chapter Four

THEY CROSSED THE RAILROAD TRACKS SOUTH of Casper a couple of hours after sunup on the fifth day and rode past the stockyards where the cattle jostled haunch to jowl waiting for their train east. "Was I right?" Bernard Pearl said. "Was that the easiest thousand anybody ever made?"

Cord turned in the saddle. Pearl jerked up on his reins, and his horse took a few contrary meandering steps before dropping its head and nuzzling the cinders along the tracks. Pearl spread one arm in a gesture that took in the lopsided barns, the tangle of rail threading through switches, the odor of curing manure on the spring air, all the fine attractions of the railroad end of any Western town. "Here we are," Pearl said proudly, as if the credit were his.

But truth to tell, the ride had been simple as eating cake, and except for Pearl's bitching and the stink of his body, pleasant as could be reasonably hoped. It felt good to ride at ease across the open greening prairie, not worrying a damn who came along, waving at the stages and buckboards and local farmer traffic, swapping a pleasant word with passing horsemen, at least those who did not give Cord and Chi a wide knowledgeable berth. Even that didn't feel so bad: Being known was a sight better than being wanted.

In more than a decade of the outlaw life they'd developed habits of caution, and generally avoided places like Casper, big enough to have organized peace officers and notions of order. Now they could ride any trail, walk into the public house of their choosing, offer a true name without worrying about facing a circle of shotgun muzzles with a posse on the other end. Cord wondered how long it would last. Maybe forever, he decided. Maybe he would grow old on his ranch, get fat as his stock, bet on race horses, and write his memoirs.

"Like stealing," Bernard Pearl said, and handed Cord $500, the second payment on their deal. Pearl wore a watery smile and seemed a little edgy, as if he wanted to get rid of them quickly as he could without being obvious.

Cord took the money and held out half to Chi. She grinned and shook her head. "You hold on to it, Cord. You're the money man in this medicine show." She waggled a finger at him. "Only don't get any ideas of running out on me."

Cord folded the fifty-dollar bills into a small square and tucked it in his watch pocket. "You sure you can get to Lawyer Meeker's by yourself, Mr. Pearl? You are not going to fall into a hole on the way, or get set upon by road agents?"

"Haw, haw. You got your money and had your joke. I'll say so long now. I got things to do."

"You ought to start with a bath, Little Stinker," Chi said.

Pearl looked at the ground and shook his head, as if he were sorely offended but too polite to make an issue of it.

"Wheew," Chi breathed. She pinched at her nose. "Pearl, you are a darling." She laughed at him. She had no use for toady men such as Pearl, except as targets for her occasionally hammer-handed jokes.

Pearl met her look for a moment before he wilted again. He kicked his tame horse to a trot in the direction of town. "Little Mouse-man," Chi called after him. She looked at Cord. "What's your pleasure, *querido*?"

"Tell you what. I been sleeping out for the better part of a week, so tonight I'm going to put up indoors. In Denver I heard about this Continental Hotel, brand-new and first-rate."

"That all you do these days, snoop around for new hotels? You going to write a guide about the finest hostelries of the West?"

"Got to give all this a try," Cord insisted. "Might not live forever. We'll have a drink, kick some ideas around."

Chi looked at him speculatively. "You aren't thinking about getting started, are you?"

"Fancy hotel man like me?" Cord was all wide-eyed innocence. "My bad days are behind me. I drink like a gentleman now, snifter or two of apricot brandy, to flavor my smoke."

"You are going soft as a spinster. Here is what I get for a partner, some *vieja*."

"I'm no old woman where it counts," Cord said. But Chi only laughed; she was as happy as he'd ever seen her. She seemed comfortable enough with ideas about settling and landowning and Montana, enough so Cord could see a glimmer of possibility that the end of this owl-hoot life might not be so far uptrail.

They left their horses in the livery stable a few buildings up the street from the stockyards and walked the three blocks to the Continental. Casper was the second largest settlement in Wyoming after Cheyenne, and like Denver, it was turning into a city, with stone buildings and as many mercantile shops as saloons. But no flower sellers, not out here on the high Wyoming plateau where the wind blew every day and hide hunters had roamed only thirty years before.

Not so many months ago, Cord would have wished for two things: some drink and a fast ride out. But these days, he anticipated each sunrise as a herald of opportunity. Soon they would ride north toward Yellowstone National Park—join in with the tourists, Cord thought, watch the ground bubble—and then into Montana. For now, he'd take the simple pleasure of walking the streets without wondering who was watching, who might recognize them and rush off to find the police.

Folks did look them over: the tall dark gunman with his creased leather saddlebags slung over his shoulder, and the handsome exotic woman with the serape and high black boots and dark radiant face. They cut a figure. Women in bonnets put their heads together and muttered out of the corners of their thin lips while sneaking little glances. Schoolchildren gaped with honest awe and pointed stubby fingers at Cord and Chi, as if they had stepped animate from the newsprint pages of the latest yellowback dime novel from Beadle & Adams. "Acting like the carnival's coming," Cord muttered.

"You're the carnival, Cord." Chi laughed.

The Continental looked first-class, a three-story Georgian brick establishment with a colonnaded facade, although the white paint of the columns was already beginning to chip where the constant wind sandblasted it. It made Cord think of Kentucky, and Kentucky made him think of Jim Beam bourbon.

"Hold up." Chi pointed down Center. Across the street and a half block down was a two-story brick townhouse fronted by a cobblestone sidewalk with a cement curb. Above a carved oak door, a shingle announced the chambers of "ROCKWELL A. MEEKER, ATTY-AT-LAW."

Pearl's boss.

"Well?" Cord said.

"*No sé*. Except that I didn't like the smell of that Pearl. I want to see..." She was off down the street before Cord could ask what. He followed her, holding his urge to get his face washed and a glass of bourbon.

"Look at the windows," Chi said when he caught up. Cord saw it then: the two upstairs and one downstairs were shuttered tight, though all along the street other shop windows and doors stood open to the mild breezy day. Not far away, the courthouse bell began to toll noon. A young man, bareheaded with short neatly combed hair and quick efficient motions, exited the Meeker chambers and locked the oak door, then rattled the knob. He was too green to be the high-powered barrister Pearl described. When Chi crossed the street and he saw her bearing down on him, he raised his eyebrows but stood his ground.

Chi said something and the young man replied. She asked a question and he frowned, and then shook his head no. Chi nodded thanks. The young man smiled and went off to his lunch.

Chi looked thoughtful when she crossed the street. "Meeker's clerk." She cocked her head at the departing young man. "That little *Perla cabrón*," she added unexpectedly.

"How's that?"

"Didn't he tell us that the lawyer sent him to Denver ten days ago?"

"Something like that."

"Meeker is taking the grand tour of Europe. He left after Christmas and returns in another month."

"Maybe Meeker sent a wire," Cord said slowly, thinking aloud. "Maybe the case doesn't come up until he gets back." Maybe anything, he thought, long as it didn't involve them.

"Maybe *Perla* is a lying son of a pig."

"Why make up a story that has so many dips and curves?"

"So it sounds true."

"All right. Forget it. I want a drink."

Chi tipped her head to one side, studying him like a mistake.

"Well what the hell?" Cord said. "Telling us lies and paying us a thousand dollars."

"I want to know," Chi said, and Cord saw there was no stopping her now.

"At least let's get rid of these saddlebags," he said wearily.

The desk clerk inside the Continental Hotel read their names upside down in the register as they signed. The names seemed to mean something, because he turned a shade paler and asked, "Staying long?"

"Eight or ten weeks," Cord said.

The clerk smiled at Cord, as if he hoped this were a joke but did not wish to laugh until he was certain.

"One night," Chi said.

"Thank you, ma'am," the clerk said. The hell with him, Cord thought—Citizen Cord, who can stay anywhere he wants, Citizen Cord who would like a drink of bourbon. One drink of bourbon.

"Have your boy take these bags to our rooms," Cord said grandly. "We got business."

"Little Mr. Pearl," Chi said. Cord sighed but nodded: first things first if you wanted peace or whiskey.

They found Pearl's horse down a side street back toward the tracks, saddled and uncared for after the long ride. The animal was hitched in front of a bar called the Fort Laramie, the sort of drinking establishment which catered to ranch hands sent to town on errands, railroad men between trains, stock tenders washing the manure-flavored dust out of their throats.

Cord and Chi pushed through the swinging doors, waited a few moments while their eyes grew accustomed to the dim light. "Over there," Chi said in a low voice. Pearl's short tight pant legs showed beneath the table in a high-sided corner booth, hitched up above his dirty white socks.

Cord and Chi weaved among the tables. Pearl was talking animatedly, bobbing forward and gesturing with his hands. He stopped as they came to stand over him, gaped, and started to rise.

The man seated opposite slapped his palm down on the tabletop. It made a sound like a rifle shot. Pearl sat down again.

The other man wore a buff Stetson with a very tall domed crown. His right hand was crimped around the handle of a beer stein. He kept his head down, so the wide brim hid his face. "You had to have yourself a drink right off. You got your horse out front, still wearing your tack. You're a damned fool." The man had a hard coarse guttural voice.

Cord knew that voice.

The man let go of the beer mug, made a fist, and drove it forward like a battering-ram. It moved no more than nine inches and caught Pearl in the middle of the face. There was a nauseating sound of crunching bone and Pearl screamed like a wounded rodent. He fell out of the booth and rolled into a ball in the dirt and spilled beer on the floor.

The man in the tall Stetson leaned out and said, "Get away from here." Bernard Pearl got to his knees and spat out blood and two teeth. He made it to his feet and staggered between the tables to the dimness at the far end of the bar. The other man looked at the smear of blood across two knuckles of his right hand. He pulled a grimy handkerchief from a rear pocket and wiped it off.

Cord shook his head. *It could not be . . .*

The man at the table finished his beer and put down the foam-streaked glass. He used one finger on the brim to push back his high-crowned Stetson and looked up at them. His face was primarily brutal, with hard mean eyes, a mirthless smile, snaggle teeth, a knife scar fading on one cheek, and a broad nose that had been broken more than once, bunched with rearranged cartilage and spiderwebbed broken capillaries. He wore neither beard nor mustache, and when he doffed his great hat in mocking deference to Chi, they saw his head was shaved to the scalp. He smiled. It was the sort of smile you might note among spectators at a dog fight, as the winner sank its incisors into the throat of the loser.

"Well now," he snarled. "Ain't this an unexpected pleasure."

Chapter Five

AT THE END OF THE BAR BERNARD PEARL WAS snuffling into a filthy towel. He wiped his face and moaned at the pain it caused, then held the towel to his broken mouth. Five customers at the bar stared down into their glasses and minded their own business. Only the bartender seemed still interested in the violent goings-on. He stood down by Pearl, three quarters of a fried ham sandwich on a white chipped plate at his elbow. He stared at the corner table, smiling vaguely, as if thinking that with action like this, he'd never need to hire any dancing girls.

Neither Cord nor Chi had moved.

The coarse man with the shaved head wore woolen trail pants held up by suspenders over a union suit, a greasy leather vest, and under his gut a gunbelt sagging with the weight of a heavy revolver. He ran his forefinger almost tenderly along the line of scar that ran from his right cheekbone straight down to his jawline. "We do not forget," he murmured.

"I remember," Chi said. "A dirty pig-son named Enos Ryker."

Ryker's hand twitched. He lowered it halfway to his hip, then changed his mind and kept the hand above the tabletop. He was in no position for gunplay, and anyway Chi was faster. Ryker knew it, but still his eyes narrowed when she drew, so quickly that no one could truthfully claim to have seen the movement, only the gun which had magically appeared in her fist.

Ryker eased the vest aside, using careful unambiguous motions. A golden star was pinned to the breast of his union suit. "I'm still U.S. Marshal, case you were wondering. You'll spend the rest of your days in the dark."

"You'll spend eternity with the worms." Chi took two steps back and tucked her pistol back under her serape. "Now it's a fair fight. Stand up, pig-man." Cord moved off to one side, and the five customers at the bar rose together, smooth as a cancan line, and elbowed out the door. Someone had been peeking.

"Now see what you done," the bartender said, as if someone had spilled a drink.

Ryker looked up Chi's gun barrel. "Sit down," he suggested. "Take a drink."

"No."

"I'm the law." Ryker had nerve, anyway. "What I say goes, and I say take a drink."

At the end of the bar, Pearl lowered the towel from his mouth and leaned forward to examine himself in the smoky glass of the mirror. His upper lip was big as a bratwurst and his nose was all over his right cheek. "Oh, Lordy," he moaned.

"You shut up." Ryker's rage was rabid, touched with the irrational. "Shut up or get out."

That looked to Cord like a fine time for Pearl to leave, but the little man shook his head, shut his mouth, and stayed put. "Awright now," Ryker said. "Just sit down and have a goddamned drink."

"We got to go," Chi said to Cord.

"You're bucking Federal law, lady."

"There's no Federal paper on us, no paper at all."

"So I heard. Too bad." Ryker kept an eye on the spot where her hands were covered. "Even so, I can jerk your strings, make life real unpleasant for you in these parts. I don't give away no weight around here." Ryker gestured and the bartender came over with glasses and a bottle each of bourbon and tequila. How did he know? Cord wondered. Was Ryker expecting them? Cord hated brainteasers.

Ryker's whole-hog craziness made Cord edgy. Cord equated survival with the ability to predict with some accuracy the actions of others; men who believed they were acting on some principle of self-interest were not hard to read. But Ryker was capable of insane rages in which, oblivious to consequences, he tried to destroy whatever rankled him, and now here he was, with all his vengeful brutishness focused on Cord and Chi.

Cord sat down. It looked like the most direct trail to defusing the moment and getting answers.

Ryker filled a shot glass with bourbon, another with tequila. Chi picked up her glass, examined the contents with a practiced eye, and poured it out on the floor. "I'm not drinking today. Bad stomach." She tossed the glass on the table. It fell on its side and rolled around on its thick false bottom. "You make me sick," she told Ryker. "I am leaving now, and you won't stop me."

She kept staring long enough to let him think about an

answer, then snorted and went through the maze of tables and out the door. Ryker and the bartender watched her go. Cord toyed with his glass but did not drink. "Did you send Pearl for us?"

Ryker turned. "Sure, he's my boy. Some story, huh?"

Cord felt his stomach clutch, as if he had reached under a rock and felt something cold but alive. "What's this about?"

"You know."

"Games."

"*My* games." Ryker thumped his chest with his fist. "My game, my rules, and I win. How do you like it?"

Cord told himself this was pointless ranting from a man gone clear to maniac.

"I've got you this time, Cord, you and your bitch. You'll get what you deserve, and I'll be there when it happens. I'll watch your faces while you piss your pants and sob."

Bernard Pearl stood at the end of the table. "Kill you dead, bastard," he lisped, staring down at Cord with livid loathing.

"I wasn't the one who knocked your teeth out," Cord said, alarmed. *Jesus, they were both bullshit*.

This was going nowhere. Cord slid out of the booth and pushed Pearl out of the way.

"Cord!" Ryker's voice was hard and demanding. "First off, you give me back my thousand dollars."

Cord walked away.

"Keep it close to hand," Ryker shouted madly at Cord's back. "I'll take it off your corpse."

Chapter Six

CORD SPEARED A ROUND SLICE OF CRISP WATER chestnut, dipped it in the pepper sauce and hot mustard he had mixed together on the edge of his plate, and munched it down. The mustard left his sinuses clear and tingling; pinpricks of sweat popped out along his hairline and made his eyes water, but he could not stop himself from dipping everything in the fiery condiments. Chi was concentrating on her plate of chop suey, shoveling beef and bean sprouts and gummy sauce into her mouth with chopsticks. Voices chattering in Chinese drifted faintly from the kitchen, but Cord felt out of sight and secure in the dimly lit booth, mostly hidden behind a folding bamboo-framed screen with wispy dragons hand-painted on rice-paper panels.

Cord wasn't much for skulking around, but truth to tell, Ryker had spooked him more than somewhat. There was no profit and enormous danger in dealing with a crazy man.

"Part of it was pure dumb luck." Cord used the wooden

ladle to scoop chop suey from a japanned bowl, poured it onto a bed of steamed brown rice. "We get our names in the paper, and Ryker sees it and has an idea. He makes up a very good story—he's crazy but he is not stupid—and sends his boy Pearl down to tell it to us." Cord stabbed a sliver of beef and considered it, on the end of his fork. "And we buy his tall tale like a fifty-cent watch." Cord dipped the beef in his hot sauce and ruminated. "It listened okay, but we didn't pay close enough attention. You get to thinking about your future life and you lose track of what's happening right now. I should have noticed, riding up here: no creeks were running anywhere near bank-full."

"Even so, the timing was too good." She carefully balanced a little stack of rice and chop suey on the ends of her chopsticks, and her eyes crossed a little as she followed the food into her mouth, snapping her jaw quickly shut as if afraid it would escape.

Cord shook his head no. "I went by the depot, talked to the agent. No creeks up, no bridges out, and a milk train comes in from Denver at nine every morning—brings a bundle of that day's bulldog edition of the *Rocky Mountain News*, too. Took us five days horseback, takes the train about that many hours." Cord raised his little porcelain cup of Chinese green tea and smiled sourly. "A toast to modern times, where you can get anywhere you want, except lost."

"Ryker reads we are in Denver," Chi said slowly, piecing it out, "about the same time we're drinking our coffee in the Brown Palace, the morning after all this started on the Post Road with those stage robbers. He also reads we don't get the reward money until the next day."

"And he knows us. We'll wait twenty-four hours for six thousand dollars every time."

"Well we did," Chi said. Cord looked up, but she shook her head a little; she wasn't blaming any of this on him.

Cord poked at his food. "There is a late train back to Denver, so Ryker had most of the day to cipher out his lie and still get Pearl to Denver by the next morning."

"Ryker!" Chi spat the name like a curse. "What is he doing around here?"

"Not a damned thing." Cord rubbed a thumbnail along his jawline. "I got a shave I didn't need. The barber talked, as barbers will. Ryker drifted into Casper with the spring. Rumors are that he picks up spare money from the big cattle interests chasing nesters out of the country—probably where he got the idea for his story. He's a U.S. marshal. He can do anything, go anywhere, and he came here."

"Our luck. What does he want?"

"Satisfaction. The question is, what is he doing about it? He knows he'd be beat if he went up against either of us in a heads-up showdown, but if he only wanted us dead he could have ambushed us off the trail. I don't know."

"Trouble, anyhow."

Cord pushed his plate away and stifled a belch. "Well sure."

Somewhere out on the street, gunfire crackled, a few pistol shots and then the sharper snap of rifles, the whine of slugs glancing off brick walls. People were shouting.

Cord and Chi sat quietly. This business began with chasing after trouble that was not theirs—except Cord had the eerie feeling this had something to do with them. Chi was already out of her seat. The bamboo-and-rice-paper screen teetered and fell. Cord went out the door on Chi's heels.

The gunfire was coming from a block up the side street where it intersected Center. Two riders came around the corner at full gallop, lying low in the saddle. Two men on foot appeared, firing pistols, and more armed men followed, a mob. Cord and Chi ducked into the cover of the restaurant's doorway recess and the riders raced past, firing blind over their shoulders.

"What the hell?" Cord yelped.

The lead rider wore a dark Stetson, leather vest, Colt .45 Peacemaker, and rode a bay gelding. The drawstring of a large canvas bag was lashed around his saddle horn.

The second rider was a dark woman in a wide-brimmed black sombrero over leather britches tucked into the high uppers of hand-tooled black leather boots. Her hair was in long black braids and she carried a second canvas bag.

"Jesus Christ." Cord stared after the riders.

It was them, him and Chi.

And they had just robbed a bank.

Chapter Seven

"**G**ODDAMN THE SCHEMING *CABRÓN*!" CHI swore.

Cord looked at her, befuddled.

But she had already seen through to the why of it. "The bastard couldn't chance murdering us in cold blood. He's a government man, has too much to lose. But now he's got us nailed into a frame, wanted for bank robbery—God knows what else—and he can ride us into the ground as he pleases, shoot us dead for resisting arrest, take his time..."

"Why?"

"You know why."

Cord thought back to another bad day with Ryker in it. But how long could a man hold a killing grudge?

"Let's move," Chi said. Cord followed her back inside and instantly a tiny Chinese woman began jabbering at them angrily. She grabbed Cord's sleeve and he gawked down at her before he got it. He stuffed a banknote into her tiny hand and pushed past down a row of screened booths into the kitchen. The tiny Oriental woman followed, plucking at the hem of his vest.

The kitchen was full of steam and exotic spicy aromas. An ancient parchment-skinned man draped in skin robes sat on a stool in the corner, drawing from a long-stemmed pipe. A man and a woman tended cauldrons bubbling atop a twelve-burner gas range, and three or four almond-eyed toddlers played at their feet. All of them stood motionless, watching inscrutably as Chi and Cord went out the back door.

Cord stopped so abruptly in the alley that Chi banged into him from behind. "Where we going?" Cord tried to gather his wits into some kind of plan.

"Hear that?" Chi said. From the direction of Center Street—and their hotel—came the swelling noise of the crowd, mindless shouting and hoorahing in search of a target. Cord was frightened. He'd seen a man killed by a mob once, in Hays City, Kansas, when he was eighteen and on his third spring cattle drive north from the Nueces River country. The man was a Mexican, a boy really, about Cord's age, and the mob got it in mind that he'd kidnapped a town woman and her two girls, beaten them and taken outrageous liberties. They stomped him to death with their boots in the middle of a back street. Cord remembered the timbre of the Mexican's scream, and his broken faceless corpse puddled in the dust. Later on, Cord heard that the woman identified her attacker, some crazy old jasper who had lived out on the prairie for years. Cord still wondered from time to time if the anonymous mobbed-up citizens of Hays still saw that Mexican boy in their nightmares. Cord did.

Cord drew a deep ragged breath and exhaled the memory

with it. "The money," he said. "Our money, in that hotel safe." Nobody was going to buffalo him to the point where he ran off and left his goods, not after all these years . . .

A man in a bowler hat stuck his head into the far end of the alley. He stared at them bug-eyed. "I got 'em cornered," the man hollered like an idiot. "Come a-running!" He reached under his waistcoat and came out with a huge colt Navy .44 with freckles of rust on the barrel and frame. He needed both thumbs to cock the hammer back; he squinted down the gun's length, grimacing with concentration.

Cord drew and bounced a shot off the brick wall a foot above the man's head; chips showered down on the man's bowler. The man yelped like a girl, dropped his weapon and ran, waving his hands over his head. But the noise of the rabid mob was getting closer, and now there was not enough money in the world to convince Cord to stand and face the crazed citizens of Casper. "We'll come back for it," Cord said. "If the hotel doesn't hold it, we'll sue, get Lawyer Meeker to plead our case."

Chi was not amused. They were in as bad a tight as they'd ever seen, caught afoot in the middle of a city, halfway lost and with no good plan, and every man in town digging his Army hogleg six-shooter out from under his old uniform to come gunning for them.

Right then it got worse. A dozen armed men came around the end of the alleyway. The smoking Colt in Cord's hand was as useless as tits on a bull. Kill a couple of citizens and he and Chi were done, no matter how this started. Enos Ryker would laugh while they kicked barefooted at the air. Someone spotted them and the animal mob cry went up. The gunning was a few seconds away, with them trapped like cut-out ducks in a carnival shooting gallery.

"*Vamos*," Chi barked, and fled, her serape flapping and her dark braids flying out from under her sombrero. Cord raced after her. They flipped over a chest-high board fence. Slugs thwacked into the planks. They ran across vacant lots and down narrow unpaved side streets. Cord held his gun butt to keep the heavy revolver from bouncing out. Getting away was the only chance; for that they would need good horses, and theirs were the best. Chi led the way; Cord hoped her fine-tempered instinct for direction worked in the city.

They zigzagged three or four blocks and the mob's lunatic cry grew fainter. They went around the corner of a canvas-walled storage shed and vaulted a two-rail fence. Half a dozen milling saddle horses stared at them incuriously. Cord drew his Colt and they edged through the back door of the livery barn.

The liveryman was a middle-aged Negro. He looked at Cord's gun and shook his head, like a man sorely tired. From the direction of downtown came faint confused shouting and occasional gunfire. Cord wondered if they had taken to shooting themselves.

"Don't you tell me," the liveryman said in a soft hush-puppy drawl. "I don't need to know nothing. I mind my business."

Cord put away his gun. Chi watched the street from the shadow of the front door. The liveryman smiled and nodded at Cord, then went to bring their horses, moving with maddening leisure. Cord paced the hard-packed dirt floor, hating this. There were times when you had to run, but recognizing them made it no more palatable.

Another black man came huffing through the front door, one strap of his overalls flapping. Cord eased back into the dimness but did not draw. "Ruffy!" The newcomer was in his twenties, with nubby short-cropped steel-gray hair. "Ruffy, they done robbed the First National Surety Bank."

"I mind my business." The liveryman's soft voice came from somewhere back among the stalls.

"Them two desperadoes that come to town." The younger man pulled a folded newspaper from the bib of his coveralls. "Them two that was writ up."

Chi came up behind him and put a hand on his shoulder. She let him see her gun but kept it pointed at the ground. Cord stepped out in front of him. "Them two right here," the young Negro said weakly.

"Give that paper here, *amigo*," Chi said mildly. They needed no more enemies in this town. "Better help the *viejo* saddle our horse. We're in some hurry."

"Yes you are," the young man said.

The newspaper was that morning's *Casper Star Tribune*. By the light spilling in at the doorway, they read the small item in the lower left-hand corner of the front page.

A WARNING TO THE CITIZENRY

From such an unimpeachable source as U.S. Federal Marshal Enos K. Ryker, recently operating out of our city, we have news of the imminent arrival of two famous road agents, the brigands known as Cord and Chi.

Drawing upon the full resources of the Government, Marshal Ryker has determined that the two outlaws will have arrived as this issue of the *Star Tribune* is published. The good Marshal points out that although the two are no longer fugitives from the law, their prior depredations will be a matter of serious regard to law-abiding citizens with the sense to take care. The people of Casper are advised by Marshal Ryker to mind their shops, homes, and personal belongings, if they do not wish to suffer. . . .

"He didn't miss a goddamned trick," Cord muttered. "Not only gets us to his town, but makes sure everyone knows we are here."

"I hate this," Chi said darkly. "Scheming, plotting fakery—worse than back-shooting, dirtier..."

"Wasn't you, was it?" The younger man came forward, staring intently up at them. "I was there; I saw 'em. I got a good eye." He laughed softly. "They was dressed like you, but their faces was pale and young." The man nodded to Chi. "Surely wasn't you, dark lady."

"Go tell the rest of them," Chi said.

The black man showed missing front teeth. "You gonna need more than one nigger's word to save your brown ass from them mopers." He cocked his head, and Cord noted the mob noise was louder and closer. He felt a chill at the base of his neck.

The liveryman led the horses out. The blankets and saddles were on loose, and Cord's travel pouch was under the man's arm. In it were matches, a little tobacco, a handful of coffee, a few other necessaries for the road, nothing valuable but all real handy on the trail—when they overnighted in a new town it stayed with the horse, against the sudden need for urgent departure. Cord tied it behind his saddle, then threw up a stirrup and tightened his cinch. "What happened back there?" he grunted.

"Them robbers come charging into that Surety Bank. There is shooting and yelling before they come out, carrying moneybags. I watched from 'cross the street. They killed a deputy town marshal from horseback 'fore they rode out, shot him dead through the heart. I saw that man fall bleeding with my own eyes."

Murdering a lawman was the worst thing you could do. Other lawmen would never let you rest except in the grave.

Cord felt like puking. Someone must have picked up their trail; the mob was getting closer.

"What you gonna do?" the black man asked.

Chi checked her cinch, then vaulted into the saddle. "Right now," she said, gathering up reins, "we are going to ride."

Cord jerked the bay's head around, ducked his head under the low doorway's lintel, and almost rode down the mob's vanguard.

There must have been a hundred of them, townspeople, ranch hands, drifters, and loafers, roaring with excitement and blood lust, a surging baying horde that had nothing to do with order, justice, or even vengeance. They wanted to see someone die, and here were killer bank robbers, materialized in their midst as if delivered by the hand of the Lord. Cord's bay gelding snorted and pranced. Cord thumped the animal, pulled on the reins. Both barrels of a shotgun went off and a chorus of men cried out in pain. Heavy pistols waved in the air, and some idiot cracked a bullwhip above his head. Wild shots echoed between the buildings, and Chi's mare half reared and kicked someone in the chest. She plunged into the crowd and Cord followed in her wake, and then they were hunched low and galloping down a side street, away from the flying lead and screaming lunacy the good people of Casper flung at their backs.

Chapter Eight

CORD HANDED THE BRASS SPYGLASS TO CHI. "I need spectacles," Cord said. "I'm seeing Indians."

Chi twisted the glass into focus. Her eyesight was keener than his. "Where the hell did he come from?"

"From nowhere. Doesn't matter. He's here."

"Right on our ass." Chi handed the glass back, and Cord squinted through it again. He lay on his belly at the edge of the rimrock along the top of a little table butte, a dozen miles out on the prairies west of Casper. They had circled to the higher ground to rest their horses a little and maybe get an idea of what sort of folk might be after them. Now they knew: about the worst sort possible.

The six riders shimmering in the spyglass lens were a couple of miles back over the endless expanse of open grassy plain, riding easily as if this were some sportsmens' jaunt. Ryker took off his dome-crowned hat and wiped at his forehead with a gray rag, his shaved pate gleaming like

brass in the afternoon sun. Bernard Pearl rode at his side,
still dressed in his clownish too-tight city clothes. Three
other gunmen rode in a rank behind them, surly-faced characters with rifles scabbarded alongside their saddles. Five
gunhands against two, and Cord and Chi's Winchesters back
in the Continental Hotel with the rest of their belongings.

The Indian did not carry a gun, according to barroom
rumor. But he read track like no other man in the West.

He called himself Mr. Earl, and was got up like a Wild
West Show caricature. He was tall, dark, well-built, with
a handsome chiseled face, but his costume was purely outlandish. Over a calico breech cloth he wore open buckskin
leggings tucked into high leather boots with folded-over
fringed tops and uppers etched with beadwork in strange
patterns that had nothing to do with any tribe Cord had ever
encountered. A serge vest that had once been part of a
business suit was draped over his hard bare chest. His black
silk top hat was half crushed so it nodded off to one side
at a crazy angle, and his long ebony braids were tied into
loops with beaded rawhide thongs. As Cord watched, the
Indian reined up and leaned down in the saddle, peered
intently at the ground through round wire-rimmed spectacles
with red-tinted lenses.

There was nothing outlandish about Mr. Earl when it
came to man-tracking. The odds had shifted anew, against
Cord and Chi. They might run but they could not hide, not
from Mr. Earl. Whatever care they took, the Indian would
read their sign like a map.

"They say he gets five thousand dollars cash in advance,"
Cord said, "and no refunds if he doesn't find your man."

"You ever hear of that happening?"

What Cord had heard was that Mr. Earl could track your
soul to Hell. Instead of answering, he said, "Where would

Ryker get five thousand dollars?" But then he knew. "God-damn the man. It's our money, out of that hotel safe."

"No it isn't." Chi had found something to grin about. "Guess I've strung you long enough." She continued. "After we ran into Ryker, I got a hunch someone had best take care of business, be ready to move." She reached under her serape and brought out their money, the $6,000 reward and Ryker's $1,000. It was wrapped into a tight bundle with twine. "Also," she said, "there is more in our name in that Tucson bank, so you can forget dying of a broken heart over money, and start concentrating on getting us out of this."

"Yeah," Cord said. "I been worrying about money like they would never print any more." Cord shook his head. He looked up at her, and found her staring flatly, as if waiting for him to wake up.

"So," she asked, "where *did* he get the money?"

"Damned if I know."

"The bank job," she said with exasperation. "You re-member: the one we've been tagged with."

Cord got it then. "Ryker has got this pieced together like a Chinese puzzle. He picks a National bank for the target, so it's a Federal crime—and him a U.S. marshal. He tells his two playactors to be certain to kill somebody—a law-man, it turns out—so there's dead-or-alive money on our heads."

"That gives him leave to kill us at leisure," Chi picked up. "He brings in the bodies, but he tells everyone there was no money on us. We must have buried it somewhere."

"Yeah. In his pocket."

"Him and the Indian."

"He's crazy as a scorpion," Cord said. He collapsed the spyglass and edged away from the rimrock. "They're only about a half hour behind us. We'd best be horseback."

He had to be crazy, Cord decided as they headed down the backside of the butte and circled around to the trail, west toward the mountains. But crazy or not, Ryker had them where he wanted for the moment, quivering at the end of his fork. He had been chewing on a grudge as if it were the food of life, for five years, and now he saw his chance to get the sour taste out of his mouth. . . .

Chapter Nine

BACK THEN CORD AND CHI RODE THE GREAT open West as if it were a set for a drama in which they were the featured players and everyone else was a supernumerary. As a consequence, they were wanted here and there, though it was rarely a matter of significant concern. Outlawry was easier in those days: you rode in, did your banking business, and rode back to nowhere. Now telegraph wires and railroad tracks went everywhere among cities and tens of thousands of people, all of them more or less devoted to a notion of societal order that viewed bank robbers dimly.

Enos Ryker was a Pinkerton operative in those days. Cord hated Pinkertons, with their offices in every goddamn place, for lying sneaks and prevaricators and strike-breaking mobsters. They were no better than bounty hunters, and in those days there was $5,000 reward money on each of them for the robbery of a Wells, Fargo express office in Durango,

Colorado. That was what got Ryker on their tail and set off this whole damned mess.

As far as Cord was concerned, the Pinkerton Detective Agency was a criminal conspiracy operating with the tacit approval of the real authorities. "Corrupt as Judas," he would say, and the worse of them was Enos Ryker. They heard stories a year before their trails ever crossed, saloon tales of how Ryker stepped all over the law on the way to his man, of how Ryker was so low he made Allan Pinkerton look like Honest Abe Lincoln.

They had been camped along the North Platte River somewhere in the sandhill country of the Nebraska panhandle. It was late August, and most of the oppressive humidity had gone out of the season. A garishly pretty sunset flared in the western sky, over where they'd find the Rockies. Cord and Chi were drifting south and west toward California for the winter, but not in any hurry and open to suggestion.

"Open to most anything," Cord would say, reflecting on those lost happy days. "Riding and hunting up something to happen." It wasn't only the money; in those days he'd been mainly seeking adventure.

There on the North Platte, Cord was building a fire of deadfall cottonwood limbs when a stranger came out of the brush down toward the water. He had his hands up by his shoulders and Chi's Colt in his back.

"Lookee here, Cord." She sounded halfway amused, halfway indignant. "This hombre was spying on me."

The stranger was about twenty years old. He had sandy hair and a bushy mustache, wore trail clothing and a broken-brimmed slouch hat. There was an empty holster on his hip and a Remington Frontier .44 in Chi's other hand. Chi tossed it and Cord caught it by the butt. Remington was going after the Peacemaker trade with this new pistol, but Cord had found the balance not to his taste. The kid looked harmless enough.

"You some kind of pervert, boy?" Cord demanded sternly.

"No," the kid said, "I am some kind of bank robber."

"Is that so?" Out of the corner of his eye, Cord saw Chi try to hide a smile. "Put your hands down," Cord told the kid. "Take some coffee. I figure you are too smart to try anything bare-handed." He cocked his head in Chi's direction. "Don't know what she figures. She likes to shoot the balls off smart-mouthed boys for sport."

The kid's name turned out to be Kyle Greer. Kyle Greer knew a bank ripe for robbing, but not a damned thing about how to go about the job.

"You never robbed a bank before?" Chi made an expression of dismay.

"Ain't never robbed nothing," Greer admitted sullenly. Then he told them about the brand new First Republic Bank in Grand Island, only in business a month and modern as they come, with time-locked, triple-walled steel vaults, silent telegraphic alarm system, two trained guards on duty all the time, everything secure as the U.S. Treasury.

"Only a fool would go up against something like that," Chi said.

The Agrarian Exchange Bank had been the only one in town, but naturally, all the big farmers and ranchers had transferred their accounts to the First Republic when it opened. With the loss in deposits, the Agrarian Exchange was struggling to stay in business. Among other economies, it had let the guard go. Not only that, but all the experienced tellers had taken better paying jobs at the First Republic. Their replacements were greenhorns, likely to turn blue and faint at the merest demand that cash-drawer contents be handed across the counter right now, before someone got shot to death. "Now there is the kind of bank to crack," Kyle Green said.

"Sure, and what for?" Chi said. "All the money is gone."

"Not all." Kyle Greer chuckled like a man who knew secrets. "Not nearly." The First Republic Bank would not receive its Federal charter for another two months. "U.S. government red tape," Greer said. "Here's more red tape," he went on. "According to Federal regulations, when military payrolls have to be held secure, they got to be deposited in a chartered bank. The payroll for the post at Fort Phil Kearney comes in to Grand Island by express car the first of each month. The escort from the Fort arrives the next day or the next to pick up the money. Meantime, guess where it abides?"

"The first of each month," Chi mused. "What day is it?"

"How would I know?" Cord said.

"I'd say it was the twenty-ninth," Greer drawled.

This sort of thing—some stranger tipping you to a sure-fire job they were aching to give away, gratis—this had happened before. But Cord liked the kid, and thought Chi felt the same. "How do you know all this, boy?"

"Starting two years ago and ending a week back," Greer said, "I was apprenticed to the head cashier."

Sipping at their coffee there by the North Platte, Kyle Greer told a story of growing up on his family's dry-land wheat farm to the south, land that never delivered much beyond blisters, sore backs, and enough food to keep from starving. One day his father was digging one of the endless series of wells which went dry soon as they were sunk, and the walls caved in on him. "Took us most of a day to dig him out," Greer said. "He was drowned in dirt."

His mother sold the farm at four bits an acre and took up hand laundering in Grand Island. "Scrubbing other people's dirty wash," Greer muttered, "while her Kyle learned a respectable calling." Ever since, he'd spent his work days ciphering columns of tiny figures and reassuring old ladies that their couple hundred dollars of life savings were safe as the vaults of Heaven.

"I was like my daddy," Greer said. "Drowning in dirt. Then my ma took sick and I had to do double time, got a night job swamping out a saloon. Something like bank work, you get my meaning. Influenza."

"What?"

"My mother had the influenza, and she wasted and died. She was a pious Christian woman, and if there is justice in the universe she is sitting on the right side of God. But right there is devout as I get. She did her best, but I never took to godly ways. When she died, I got a little house and fifty-seven dollars, but mainly I got free."

Cord sensed the boy was feeling a little guilty, but that was irrelevant to the major topic of discussion. "So you decided to rob your own bank. You're some thinker, boy."

"That's right," Greer said. "I been thinking plenty. I saw my fortune in the big city—fact is I was riding for Denver when I spotted the two of you coming through Julesburg. Your pictures are in more banks than the President's."

Greer smiled into his coffee cup. "Two years of working with other people's money and I never thought of taking a penny, but seeing you, I come to a great discovery. Take a penny, take it all.

"I got ambitions," Greer said. "I don't want to die in a collapsed well nor live under the thumb of no bank. I want to travel around, see the sights, explore opportunities..."

As the boy talked on, Cord recalled his own early days on that dry-land patch in southeast Texas, how quickly he had run when he'd had the chance. "First thing is money," Greer said. "A man ain't shit without money." He looked up, shook a finger. "And this here is Army money, Government money. We ain't gonna steal some old lady's purse."

"It's money, that's all," Chi said. "Ours, if we take it."

"That's right," Greer said, happy as a proctor whose student has just grasped a particularly abstruse lesson. "We have ourselves a deal."

As it happened, they did, and the bank job came off smooth as glass. They rode into Grand Island two days later, a few minutes before three on a fragrant drowsy Friday afternoon. On the farms and ranches spread across the prairie, men worked and sweated and stared at the sky for some hint of rain cloud. In town few people were abroad. The business of the week had been wrapped up early, and the Army payroll was safe for the weekend in the Agrarian Exchange Bank, awaiting Monday and the escort from Fort Kearney.

It was a single-story stone building in the old part of town, near the river and the stockyards, sharing a street corner with a hardware store, a vacant lot, and an old abandoned homesteader's cabin that was left over from the pioneer days and was too much effort to tear down. The better part of town had moved further up the bluffs. Back of the bank was a workingman's boarding house that had once been a traveler's hotel. A narrow alleyway ran between the buildings to a back street that would deliver them to the main road west out of town.

Greer was horse holder, with orders to stay out of sight. Cord and Chi were already wanted by plenty of law, but there was no need for Greer to get tagged with a part in this, assuming all went well.

Cord came out of the alley on foot and crossed to the shade of the hardware store's awning. He watched a man exit the bank, touching his hat to Chi as she went in past him. The man stared at where she'd been for a moment, then shook his head; a notion had flitted through his mind and been instantly rejected as being as likely as resurrection. The man tucked his money into his billfold, his billfold into his coat pocket, and went off briskly toward the center of town.

Cord saw Chi behind the stenciled window. She nodded. He crossed the street and entered the bank. The big-faced Roman-numbered clock on the wall above the tellers' counter read one minute to three.

There were no customers. The two tellers, young men in tinted celluloid visors, striped shirts, and arm garters, were toting up the day's transactions. Behind the cage-railed counter in an office area was a vacant desk and beside it an easel and a high stool, at which the head cashier made entries in a ledger book. He was an aged turkey-necked geezer with a long beak upon which pince-nez glasses perched delicately as a butterfly. He frowned at Cord; here was a man who spent good cheer frugally. Kyle Greer's boss; it was a wonder the kid had lasted long as two years. A mother's love, Cord thought, and a son's wish to please.

Chi's lever action Winchester came out from under her serape. Cord drew his .45 and showed it to the tellers. "Grab some sky," Cord said. Behind him, Chi snorted. A couple nights earlier, he had been reading to her from a Deadeye Dick novel, and the line was Deadeye's. The tellers didn't get the joke. They raised their hands and stared stupidly. The old cashier opened his mouth and clamped it shut, jarring his pince-nez from his nose. He caught it in a cupped palm. A walk-in vault was set into the wall behind him, and to one side was an oak door.

Cord came around the end of the counter. "Open that vault."

The cashier replaced the pince-nez and examined Cord through it. "Only Mr. Farley can open the vault," the old man said irritably, as if everyone knew about Mr. Farley. He dipped his head at the oak door.

It opened at that moment to admit a jowly, roly-poly little capitalist with a black suit and a red face. "What goes on?"

Chi came around the counter behind Cord. "Open the vault, *Señor* Farley." Cord stepped back to cover the tellers and the scrawny cashier.

Farley drew himself up to his full stature of five feet three inches. "I will not."

Chi shrugged. "Kill him," she said to Cord.

Cord pursed his lips and shook his head. "I don't know," he said reluctantly.

"Never mind," Chi snapped. "I'll do it." She levered a cartridge into the breech of her Winchester, jammed the muzzle into Farley's gut, and cocked the hammer.

Farley gasped and scuttled to the vault.

Cord fought to keep a straight face. This was an old time-saving gag that hadn't failed yet. To the typical banker, Chi was alien as an Ethiopian, and maybe crazy enough to kill in cold blood. From there on the bank job was incidentless as a poem. Farley opened the vault and they rode north out of Grand Island with more than $10,000. By nightfall they were well on the other side of the Loup River, and that night they drifted into a sleep easy as well-suckled babes.

Cord was snoring softly and dreaming of rosy ladies in barroom paintings coming to life when the cold muzzle of a double-barreled shotgun jabbed painfully into his forehead.

Cord opened his eyes and held his breath. He saw a canopy of cottonwood branches, stars peeking through their heavy leaves. He lowered his eyes. A thick stocky bulk moved back and the pressure of the shotgun eased. Cord sat up and exhaled. It felt like two or three in the morning.

The man with the shotgun removed a high-crowned Stetson. His shaven head gleamed in the starlight. "You know me."

"Ryker," Cord muttered.

"Pinkerton *cabrón*." Chi was off to one side where Kyle Greer, the turncoat son of a bitch, was covering her with his Remington Frontier .44. She turned on him, ignoring the weapon. "And you, you son of a whore." Greer winced at the insult to his mother. "You ought to be ashamed of yourself," Chi scolded. "You pretended to be my friend."

Chi slapped Greer's face, a hard stinging blow that left her livid handprint on his cheek. Miraculously, no one shot her.

"No more of that now," Ryker ordered. "Get on your feet," he told Cord.

"My revolver is rolled in my poncho." Cord cocked his head at his makeshift pillow. "Wanted you to know, so you don't get excited when you find it and do something I'd regret."

"Nothing is going to happen. No accidents anyway." Ryker spooked a man, his brutal face under his big-domed hat. He looked like a circus ape dressed in man's clothes.

An ape with all the guns. Cord stared at Greer. "You pleased with yourself, boy? You going to think back fondly on this night?" Cord had a hunch that the kid was less than totally committed to these proceedings. He might be their only hope.

"You shut up," Ryker snapped. Perhaps he sensed his weak side lay with the boy. "We are going down to the river now."

"What for?" It was Greer.

"You keep your counsel, boy." Ryker waved the shotgun at Cord and Chi. "Now move."

They led the way down a deer trail toward the water. The Federal money on them was dead-or-alive, and this crazy bald-headed Pinkerton son of a bitch meant to collect the easy way.

Only first there was the entertainment.

The trail ended in a clearing amid the willows, a little grassy beach. The water of the Loup River glinted with points of starlight. Ryker held the shotgun on them and Greer stood a little to one side with his revolver. He was frowning and trying to swallow what was coming next.

"Get away from your boyfriend a mite," Ryker said, gesturing with the double-barrel. Chi took a couple of steps toward the water.

"Now, you want any chance of survival, you start stripping out of them Mexican duds. Show me that you are too fancy to kill, *chiquita*."

"This isn't right," Kyle Greer said.

"You don't like it, get the hell out of here." Ryker kept his eye on Chi. "Strip 'em off."

Chi did not move for a long time. Finally her hands went to the brim of her sombrero. Ryker watched like a hobo at a bakery window.

"He's going to kill us anyway," Cord said conversationally to Greer. The kid was fascinated as Ryker by Chi's slow hypnotic moves. "How long you been a Pinkerton, boy?"

Ryker did not seem to hear. Chi pulled the rawhide thong up over her chin and took off the sombrero.

"Ain't no Pinkerton," Greer said sullenly. "I work for him."

"Bull," Cord said. "Like the rest of your story."

"No. Everything I told you was true, about my mother and working for that hawk-nosed cashier."

"Only you left out one thing," Cord said coldly.

"Stand away from him, Cord," Ryker barked from near the water. "You keep that goddamned gun on him, boy."

"You going to have Kyle here pull the trigger on us, Ryker?" Cord called.

Ryker smiled at Chi. "This scattergun holds a load for each of you. What washes ashore downriver is gonna look like gunny sacks of raw meat. The hogs'll strip your bones clean." Ryker snapped his fingers. Chi drew her serape over her head and dropped it on the grass.

"You think on this, boy," Cord said to Greer, his voice low and hard. "That crazy man yonder is your fit partner, and he is fixing to murder us—soon as he finishes his other nasty business. And you are just as big a part of it, killing for money."

"You say," Greer challenged. "All them banks you robbed."

"Read the posters. Not one says a damned thing about killing. We got only one murderer here—two, unless you stop this."

"Greer!" Ryker's voice sounded hoarse. "Fetch me your revolver. I'll hold it until this is done with, keep you from getting involved."

Greer did not move.

"Boy, you give me that gun." Ryker's tone was low and menacing as a grizzly's growl. He kept his eyes and the shotgun on Chi.

"I don't think I will," Greer said.

Ryker turned his head for a second to flash a furious look at Greer. Chi was on Ryker's back instantly, moving quick as chance in the silvery starlight. She threw her weight forward and they were on the ground, wrestling for the shotgun. Ryker got half turned and Chi put a knee hard between his legs. His breath exploded in a moaning sigh and the end of this was past doubt.

All of this happened in a second or two. As Chi jumped Ryker, Cord chopped the side of his left hand into Greer's wrist. The Remington fell to the ground and Cord went after it, rolled, and came up with the gun cocked and on Greer, who appeared paralyzed by this sudden unpleasant turn in his country-boy fortunes.

Chi was liable to blow a huge hole in Ryker's middle at any moment. Her eyes glowed with feline intensity and she was rigid with terrific anger. Cord tensed in anticipation of the roar and the fiery blast, but then Chi tossed the shotgun to him. He was startled and caught it awkwardly by the stock. Right now Chi was spooky as Ryker.

She retrieved the serape and shrugged into it. "*Muchacho*," she said without looking at Greer, "you ride out of here. Do it quick, before my temper goes."

"Get yourself horseback, boy," Cord said under his breath.

"Hold up." Greer shook his head, coming back to himself. "I ought to have a share. Nobody would have any money if it wasn't for me."

"*Pendejo*," Chi spat. She stalked over, wrenched the shotgun away from Cord, and blew off a barrel into the ground at Greer's feet. Flame like lightning spewed from the muzzle, and pellets thwacked into Greer's boots and his shins. He yelped and stumbled away into the trees.

Chi's anger was building like surf when the wind freshens, and Cord wondered whether he would get her stopped before Ryker was dead, and how much he cared. Except that what they did not need out of this was a dead Pinkerton. Cord heard Greer's hoofbeats recede into the darkness.

"You want to play funny games?" Chi said to Ryker. He

backed away toward the water, his hands up. "We will play some games."

She backed Ryker up to a thick, gnarled willow trunk, then threw down the shotgun and bound his hands behind him with a leather thong. Cord kept Ryker covered, but by now the bullet-headed detective was incapacitated by his own fear.

Chi drew her knife and smiled. Cord felt a little sick in his stomach.

She skinned his clothing off delicately as a surgeon. She cut his suspenders and slit his britches up both legs and peeled them away, and then she did the same with his union suit, the knife whispering through cloth and never touching skin. Ryker stood in the starlight naked except for his boots. His belly was thick and white and puffy.

"Let's go," Cord said.

"All right," Chi said pleasantly. "We're mostly done here." She laughed and turned and took a step toward Cord, and then she spun like a duelist and her knife ripped down the flesh of Ryker's face.

Ryker screamed and the flesh over his cheekbone parted in a perfect straight line from below his left eye to his jawline, a three-inch slit welling blood. It dribbled over his chin like drool and plinked onto his bare chest.

"Jesus," Cord breathed. All their years together, and still she could shock and frighten him.

Chi waved the bloody knife in front of Ryker's eyes. "You'll wear my mark for life, *cabrón*. You will see my brand every time you pass a mirror. I'll tell everyone what happened."

"Bitch." Flecks of blood flitted in the air, and Ryker began to blubber like a child.

"Time to ride," Cord said neutrally. He did not want to set her off again.

But Chi smiled mildly enough. "Sure. That might do me good, a quiet ride under the stars."

Cord took a last look at Ryker, weeping and tied up naked in his own blood and filth. Good enough, Cord decided. They broke camp quickly and saddled the horses, and were on their way within minutes. At the last, Ryker was bawling and howling like a slobbering rabid dog.

Time and again, here and there, they heard stories. Six months after their run-in, Ryker was fired from the Pinkertons for trying to work some dirty setup or another; that much was true fact. Other tales listened less well: Ryker had turned outlaw, or bounty hunter, or regulator for a big land company near Red Bluff, California. Cord and Chi paid minimal attention; there was no career in worrying over the Enos Rykers of the world. Looking over your shoulder all the time kept you from seeing the way ahead.

Then, a couple of years back, there were articles in the papers about Ryker being appointed a U.S. Marshal by the President. Cord figured Ryker bribed some Senator, or maybe ran a little blackmail. Either way, Ryker began to gather up a small sort of reputation, for manhunting and ruthlessness. Cord remembered a broadside with a photograph of the three murdering Barnabas brothers, laid out on shingles neat as a string of trout. "The law has seen fit to post these men dead or alive," Ryker told some reporter, "and I never gainsay the law."

Ryker went on bringing in men cold as winter, and crowing to the newspapers. He took to announcing to the reporters whom he would pursue next, called it "giving fair warning." He generally got his man anyway, because he spent money on stoolies, turncoats, and stupid boys like Kyle Greer.

Cord noted with passing interest that Ryker never mentioned him or Chi in his boasting, but didn't put any stock in it one way or the other. They stayed clear of him as they would any U.S. Federal marshal. Ryker was one of many law-dogs and bounty men determined to convert their hides to fame and cash money.

Now, riding west of Casper across the Wyoming prairie toward sundown and the distant mountains, Cord considered that they had underestimated the depths of Ryker's hatred. He had never crowed about catching them because it was for him a personal matter, and he wished them to die in special horrible ways. Cord saw Ryker tied to the willow in the bright summertime starlight, naked from the boot tops up, and Chi with her knife, slashing at him. Enduring that could turn a man crazy with hate, narrow the mind's view until it saw nothing but vengeance.

Cord put his pondering aside. Only one thing mattered now: Ryker was two miles back and going to kill them, barring luck or a good idea.

Chapter Ten

IF THERE WERE A WAY OUT, IT LAY WEST, across the open empty country to Wind River and beyond into the gulch-cut foothills of the east slope of the Divide. Riders could fold away into such territory and be gone forever, maybe even from a tracker of Mr. Earl's skill. It was the one best chance for now.

In the waning light of a purple sunset, Cord and Chi were crouched over a fold-creased map of Wyoming Territory. Chi had won it in a poker game in Laramie three years before. Military maps were worth more than money when you were moving through strange country, because they were sketched in relief to show the lay of the land off the trails; this one was based on Fremont's survey of 1843 and the work of other government topographers since then. With his guide Kit Carson, Fremont had camped not far from where Cord and Chi were holed up. The land was the same, except now it was mostly claimed, and bound by lines on paper.

They were twenty or so miles west of Casper, in a copse of stunted juniper along a nameless trickle creek. During the afternoon they had gained another mile or so on Enos Ryker. A few minutes earlier, from above their position on the edge of a high prairie ridge, Cord had watched the posse through his spyglass, Mr. Earl bent over in his saddle reading track in the last light, Ryker back a length out of his way, Bernard Pearl and the three sour-faced gunmen, all coming on in the shimmering heat and hanging dust.

Cord was worried about the horses, from a point of view of survival rather than sentimental attachment. In this situation, nothing counted so heavily as the ability to keep moving. The long-reached Standard Bred/Morgan crosses they rode were strong as any breed in the West, but limited like any horse by the boundaries of pure endurance. Push hard enough in this endless Wyoming high desert and the animal would give all it had, feather out and fail. There was nothing to do but ease along and stay low, take water where you could and hope you had time and horse stamina to reach mountains and lush pasture.

It would have been a pleasant enough spring evening, the air warm and still and crickets whirring in the brush, the sun touching the rolling treeless horizon. Chi stood. "He thinks he's got us. That son of a pig Ryker thinks he had us roped and trussed and ready for gutting. We might have to stand our ground, fort up, and have it out."

Cord folded the map and stuck it inside the travel pouch behind his saddle. "Not yet," he said. "We fort up now and all he has to do is wait us out."

"We got water here."

"Fine, except we'd be eating field mice in short order."

Cord fished his pouch from his flapped shirt pocket and handed it over.

"There are ways this could work out." Chi creased two papers and balanced them between her fingers, sprinkled tobacco in a thin even line, and pulled the drawstring closed with her teeth.

"Tell me a good one."

Chi licked the brown paper daintily, twisted the smokes closed, and handed one to Cord. "We search out those two who made out they were us," Chi said. "Track them and the money down and make them tell their story. We're clear."

Cord struck a lucifer on the sole of his boot and lit both smokes. "What do we do with the money?"

Chi looked exasperated. "We give it back."

"Give back the money?" Cord echoed incredulously.

"Cord, we have got plenty of money." Chi was trying to be patient. "We don't want money. What we want is to not get sucked back into the old days, with us always on the run. You and I have come to agree on that one thing, at least."

Cord blew smoke out into the twilight. "We sure as hell are on the run at the moment. Will be, I guess, long as Ryker is alive."

"Don't you see it, *querido*?" Chi said urgently. "Ryker was afraid to shoot us down in cold blood—otherwise why would he have bothered with this dog-and-pony show? And he still is afraid. He can't risk pure murder. So if we find those other two, turn them and the money in, and make sure they own up to the truth, we are clear as we were before this storm started."

"No," Cord said. "Goddamn it, no!" He turned away. The moon was edging up over the eastern horizon and the brightest stars were beginning to dot the blue-black sky.

"Nobody is going to sneak up on us. Ryker is camped for the night by some creek, bet on it. They got all the time in the world, that's what Ryker figures. There is no rush."

Chi was looking at him strangely. "What do you mean, 'no'?"

Cord watched the moon. "Ryker is crazy."

"*Loco*. Sure. Of course."

"I mean really crazy." Cord turned back to her. "He is high-centered on the idea of running us into the ground and stomping our brains into some mud hole. That cut on his cheek is festering and sending poison to his brain. He can't get over what you did to him."

"He deserved worse."

"I'm not gainsaying you on that. But we've been down this trail before, and we know how it has got to come out."

Chi nodded, but let him talk it out.

"Unfinished business," Cord said. "It won't ever go away. This sort of trouble from some earlier time sticks to you until you take care of it. You can duck it for a time but you can't outrun it, especially when it gets close. Something like Ryker and his little posse out there." Cord gestured at the night. "They will take their time and stick to us like trail dogs, unless we get rid of them once and for all."

"You thinking about killing him?"

"Maybe," Cord said. "Ryker has some bad news coming to him. Maybe we are it."

"Killing a lawman..." Chi began.

Cord threw down his cigarette butt and ground it into the scrub grass under his boot heel. "We're already wanted for killing a lawman, that poor bastard of a deputy town marshal back in Casper. So, *no sé, compadre*. You tell me how we are going to get out from under that killing, *and* get Ryker off our backs for good. You want to fix it so we can move on to Montana and maybe some kind of god-damned real life for once. You think up a plan, *amiga*."

Cord stalked off into the darkness without giving her a chance to respond. He was not angry at her, of course, just filled to bursting with rotten luck. Why did this craziness have to intrude now, when everything seemed on the verge of working out? Running outside the law was close to im-possible now, and Cord for one was willing to give it up, if they would only let him. Over time, the blood cooled and the mind no longer fixed itself on the same reckless objec-tives.

It was childish to moan, Cord decided, calming down. When you rode beyond the law for ten years you couldn't expect your past to dissolve like salt in water. But damn, this business of becoming a law-abiding citizen was more complicated than he'd reckoned. . . .

Chi was crouched on her haunches, finishing her smoke, when he returned. "Doesn't take much to light you off, does it?" she said. "A murder charge and posse on your tail, and you go all to pieces."

"Your idea of finding those two imposters," Cord said carefully. "There's a problem or two there. They could have lit out in any direction once they were clear, even circled back to Casper. They are maybe having a drink there right now, laughing their asses off. Dump those stage costumes in some gully, ride in, and order a beer. Who says there is no such thing as the perfect crime?"

"The only ones who can call them liars and make it stick is us, and we are gone for a while, thanks to that bastard Ryker."

"So what do we do?"

Chi shrugged. "Get some rest, like you say. This is as good a place as any. We can see a few miles, and we're safe long as we keep a guard."

A horse whinnied and snorted: Cord's gelding, hobbled and grazing down by the creek. The sound carried clear and far in the thin cooling night air. Cord crouched and duck-walled up to the ridge. There was a lone rider on the trail from the west, maybe a quarter mile off, reined up and head cocked in a listening posture.

Chi came up beside him. "Does he know we're here?" Cord whispered. The rider's horse nickered, and Cord's gelding snorted again in response.

"Does now," Chi said.

"I'll cover you," Cord said, and edged back from the rim. Prudent folk did not generally ride this wild country after dark unless they were sneaking around, but that did not mean this represented danger to them. Assuming a person did have legitimate reason to be abroad, he'd likely ride in, seeking coffee, and a few minutes of gab.

Which did not obviate the need for caution. Cord moved down through the low brush to the horses, while Chi came out where she could be spotted. The rider waved and turned in the direction of their cold camp. Cord circled around by the creek, cropping to hands and knees to crab-walk to the edge of the clearing. Chi was facing the visitor, whose back was to Cord.

Chi's hands were under her serape, and her expression was neutral. The rider wore a rubberized poncho. "You're not riding alone." The rider had a curious high voice. "Where's your man?" The rider turned slightly and Cord saw the gun.

Cord rose and eased forward on cat feet, put his Colt on the rider's back. "You found me," he said. He came up close enough to touch the gun to the poncho. "First you drop the gun."

The revolver hit the grass.

"Next, hands up high. Then turn around. Everything happens very slowly."

The rider turned. It was a woman, a girl really.

"*Mi hermana.*" Chi sounded as if she found this amusing.

Cord stared into the girl's face and saw the vague resemblance. But Chi's sister? What the hell . . . ?

"*Mi hermana* the bank robber," Chi said.

"Well I'll be dipped," Cord said.

"Put up your gun and sit," Chi said. "*La hermana* has a story to tell."

Chapter Eleven

"FIRST OFF," CORD SAID, "LET'S GET THE HELL out of here."

"Take her?" Chi cocked her head.

Cord scowled at the girl in the rubberized poncho. "Got to, for now."

Chi nodded. Cord jammed his Colt back into its holster, but after that no one moved. This was happening too quickly. This business kept taking disconcerting turns, and Cord hated the feeling that other people were pulling his strings. "You let her get the drop?"

Chi's hand came out from under her serape. The girl's eyes widened at the Colt that had been covering her all along. "I was curious," Chi said. "Still am. So you are with us for a while, *hermana*." Chi wagged the Colt's barrel. "Climb back on your horse."

"We can be friends," the girl said. "We are working for the same ends."

"Sure, *amiga*," Chi said. "Now get on your horse, or we will tie you on like a sack of grain."

"You got no call..."

Chi took two quick steps and put her revolver in the girl's face. "*Bizcochita*," Chi hissed. "I got all the call in the world. You put me in the middle of this trouble. You never saw me before, didn't know a damned thing, but just the same you robbed a bank and killed a lawman, and I am the one they want to hang. So you step carefully, and weigh every word you say to me."

"I didn't kill anybody. Ryker is your man."

"Maybe, but right now I got you. So you move your ass, *pronto*."

"You don't have to run," the girl said petulantly, like a child forced to bend to the illogic of an adult's will. "Ryker won't come after you in the dark—doesn't have the men for it. The big Indian don't get paid to lift a gun. Them three Payne cousins aren't worth spit, and you know Pearl."

Chi scowled. She hated for people to know things she did not, especially things about her. And how did this girl come by her helpful information, and why was she handing it out free?

"Ryker means to ride you down," the girl went on. "He wants you tied up and looking into his ugly face when he uses that shotgun on you." She poked her chin out at Cord. "She'll be first, so you can watch. That's what Ryker likes to say, heard him myself. The Devil is in that man," she added surprisingly.

Chi stepped away and lowered the gun, but kept it in her hand. "What's your name?"

"Kelsey."

"What do you want, *Señorita* Kelsey?"

"Your guns." The girl smiled a little, as if things were finally beginning to go her way. "Your guns, on my side."

"Whose side is that?"

"Not Ryker's."

"What are you trading?" Cord asked.

"A way out of this, for you."

"*Bueno*," Chi said sourly. "Which way is that?"

The girl called Kelsey crouched suddenly on her haunches. The rubberized poncho tented around her. She pulled up a handful of grass and let the blades dribble between her fingers, then stared at their pattern as if casting their fortunes. "First thing," she said in a low expressionless voice, "you got to kill Ryker."

Chapter Twelve

*D*AMN, CORD THOUGHT, *BUT WOULDN'T COFFEE go fine.* Or whiskey; bourbon whiskey would go even finer. But they didn't have whiskey, nor any other comforts such as their Winchester rifles. The girl Kelsey was carrying ground beans and a pot, but Cord was damned if they were going to risk a fire.

So Cord drew on a cigarette and thought his dark thoughts, about the snake-crazy Ryker and his queer little lapdog Bernard Pearl, and the Indian tracker named Mr. Earl, in his circus-clown costume and round red glasses. Except there was nothing funny about any of them. Cord stared balefully through cigarette smoke at the girl and wondered where she fit in and how she skewed the overall odds.

She was younger than Cord had first thought, probably not yet twenty. The rubberized poncho covered her to the knees, and below she wore mud-splattered denim pants. Her boots were worn and the heels turned over. When she swept aside the voluminous skirts of the poncho, she was tiny, an inch or two over five feet, and she had a gamine's little-boy body.

Atop dark, straight hair cut short in shapeless and severe bangs, she wore a crushed slouch hat with a narrow round crown and a broken floppy brim, the hat of a muleskinner or a farm girl but rarely of a dashing desperado. Overall she could have used a wash, but so could they all.

But she had a strong handsome little face, open-featured with a small turned-up nose and dark quick eyes and white even teeth. Cord thought she might be Italian or Hebrew, or even part Indian. A good enough kid, Cord sensed, but unsure of herself in this high muddy water and struggling to keep her footing.

"Girl, what happened to those fine duds you wore in Casper?" Cord gestured at her boots. "You like those boots better than the hand-tooled boots Ryker fitted you up with?"

"I don't like anything Ryker touches," Kelsey snapped. "But I'm not stupid—you ought to get used to that idea right off, if we're doing business. Anyway, them boots and leather britches and that braided horsehair wig, they are wrapped up with a rock inside the serape, rotting at the bottom of the North Platte River. No one is ever going to hook me up with that bank robbery."

"How about me?" Chi said darkly.

"Not you either. Not if you are smart."

"I'm smart enough." Chi bit off the words. "If you say different, I'll bloody your mouth for you. You got me into this trouble and then you ride in and expect to get welcomed like money from home. So you be smart as me, watch your mouth, and maybe you might live another hour or two."

The girl wet her lips with the tip of her tongue.

"I'd be in the right if I killed you," Chi said. "By my

lights, anyway." Chi frowned, but her tone softened. "Think before you speak, *hija*."

Somewhere off north a train rumbled and clattered through the night. Cord recalled the hatched line of the tracks on the military map. "Tell me about Ryker," he said. "Tell me why you are so sure he isn't sighting a rifle on the spot between my shoulder blades, right this minute."

"Ryker doesn't have to sneak around." Kelsey seemed relieved at the chance to get out of the heat of Chi's glare. "He's been making money on the side, as some marshals will, working as a regulator for the big cattle companies."

"Doing what?"

"Scaring nesters. The cattlemen broadcast the news that Ryker is working on their behalf, and all he needs do is come calling and look mean. The nester wets himself, and fences come down. Ryker rides on his reputation—he don't hardly ever need to gun down any sodbusters these days."

Kelsey cocked her middle finger and flicked her cigarette into the darkness. "So you see how it is. Ryker has got friends on the big ranches. Any direction you run, he has fresh horseflesh. Change animals every day if he wants. He'll follow you until yours drop dead, and by then you'll be tired and careless too. Right away he will be at your throat, like a pack dog going for a mule deer."

Kelsey threw her hands in the air. "He has all the time in the world. He can go where he wants and do what he pleases, all legal. He is a U.S. marshal."

"What would they say," Chi suggested, "if we brought you back to Casper, made you tell the law what you just told us?"

"They'd say you were liars—after they finished laughing—and throw your ass in jail to wait for hanging."

She stood abruptly, and Cord automatically shifted a little to his left to free his gun. "Ryker tells a whale of a tall tale," Cord said. "How do we know you are not playacting a role in one of them?"

"Think what you want, but hear me out. Take your chances. I sure as hell am."

That was true enough, Cord had to admit.

"I came to you," Kelsey pointed out. "I heard how you been partnered up all these years. You trusted each other so long, I figure I can trust you too. Got me a partner of my own, you know."

Another too-quick turn. "How's that?" Cord said.

"Been together over two years," Kelsey said, a little dreamily. "Not doing so bad neither."

"At what?"

"This and that. We rustled some cows, even robbed a stage or two."

"You're not sure exactly how many?" Chi put in.

Kelsey smiled at her. "Anyway we was doing all right, until Ryker came back. Crazy egg-sucking bastard." She looked up quickly, like a child surprised at her own brashness, and not sure what reaction it would draw.

"Maybe you are not cut out for this line of work, *hermana*," Chi said.

"Funny thing is," Kelsey said, "you're right. I want out. Me and my partner, we been getting on good. Like husband and wife, if you know what I mean." She lowered her head, and Cord thought he saw color high on her cheekbones. "But I'm not so tough, and my partner, he's . . ." She looked up. "He's not always right, especially if I'm not there to take care."

Cord wasn't sure what that meant, but before he could ask, Kelsey spit out the rest in a burst. "We was ready to settle down, but then there was Ryker again. He had us good."

"How do you mean?"

"He knows something that can hurt us, me and my partner. Something bad, I won't tell what. Bad enough so we are only free if he is dead."

"Something like us, maybe," Cord muttered. Chi pursed her lips but did not contradict him.

"I can give him to you," Kelsey said urgently. "I can put that Enos Ryker in your gunsight."

"How did you find us?"

Kelsey shook her head impatiently, as if that were not to the point. "After we robbed that bank we rode west out of town. You guessed right, and I spotted you on our trail ten miles out of town, maybe less. I got good eyes. I didn't tell my partner."

"Why not?"

"Never mind that now. What happened was we made camp and after he was asleep, I doubled back."

"Your partner must sleep like death."

"He was drinking."

"Sounds like it," Cord said. "So you rode out on him."

"I left a note. We'd fixed on a place to meet if something went wrong and we got split up. I told him I'd be there, sometime tomorrow."

"Be where?"

"I'm not telling." Kelsey went on quickly. "Not until you agree to my plan. I will lead you to my partner, and once he learns you are dead against Ryker he will throw in with us, because he can't do nothing else. He is in thrall to the man, and must get free."

"Keep to the track, girl," Cord said sharply. "What do we do once we get to your secret place?"

"We wait. Mr. Earl will follow our sign, lead Ryker into our trap. We'll be four guns by then, rifles too, and we will slaughter them, like shooting hogs in a sty." She smiled at the picture.

She was a mite changeable for Cord's taste. "That leaves us one step back of where we started," he said. "Still wanted for robbery and murder, with an extra dead lawman tossed in."

"Tell me a better plan, Mr. Cord," Kelsey said with surprising vehemence. "You got no hole card, you two. There may be some way you can get away from Ryker for good and true, and clean clear of the murder charge to boot, but I don't see it. And another thing you don't want to hear . . ."

"Then don't say it," Chi snapped.

Kelsey did not even look at her. "Ryker means to kill you. So you got to settle it once and for all, because till then you are walking dead. Every time you turn a corner, there is Ryker with his finger on the trigger of that sawed-off shotgun. He won't forget."

Cord was startled: did she know about that first meeting between them and Ryker, five years back? "Enough," he said.

"Make the best of a bad situation," Kelsey suggested, and went to see to her horse.

Cord stared after her. The girl took some dizzying turns. "We'll move on," Cord decided. "A few more miles, so we know we are making the effort." He smiled weakly at Chi to take the tension off.

"And *mi hermana*?"

"For now she is with us." Cord watched the girl check her cinch. "I think better in daylight." He went down to the creek and got the bay and the mare, still saddled as a precaution against rude surprises.

"You do need me, you know," Kelsey said as he passed.

"Don't be a nuisance," Cord said. He checked his own cinch and Chi's, then swung into the saddle. Stars speckled the cloudless sky.

Kelsey paused with her left foot in the stirrup. "There is one more piece of news you should know: we did not kill that deputy town marshal." She looked at the stars, as if the constellations illustrated the scene in her mind: the aging lawman's chest exploding with blood and then the frozen moment when he lay facedown in the street.

"Ryker ordered us to kill somebody," Kelsey said. "A lawman if we could. We told him to go to hell. We wanted no part of that. So Ryker rigged up a pistol support and hunted up a spot on the roof of the dry goods store across the street from the bank, did the deed himself. It was only a thirty-foot shot, and in all the brouhaha nobody noticed where it came from. But I saw him there, the moment before he killed that deputy. I had an eye on him, case he decided to go for us."

She climbed onto her horse. "My partner and me, we may not be all white, but we never killed nobody."

"That's a comfort," Cord said, but he happened to believe she was mostly telling the truth. She had to be, or they were all fried.

Chapter Thirteen

HOURS LATER, AS THE MOON WAS TOUCHING down to set, they cut the Bridger Trail where it swung north of the breaks country known as Hell's Half Acre. Casper was some fifty miles to their back now, and Cord was considering the wisdom of halting for shut-eye. Neither they, nor the horses, could keep up this pace much longer— especially them, Cord thought tartly, listening to his muscles groan and his joints creak. Getting old, he thought, old and soft. Bridger was sixty the year he mapped this route, romping in the saddle like a youngster. Had three wives one at a time, all Indian. Maybe there was strength in that part of it, the women . . .

A horse length ahead, Chi and the girl Kelsey rode side by side, leaned in their saddle with heads close together. Cord heard the murmur of their low voices but could not make out the words. Chi had been hard on the girl, but that was Chi's way of cutting through the crap to any real threat, if it existed. Apparently Kelsey had passed the test.

Chi was taking the girl under her wing. Cord had seen it happen before. A couple of winters earlier it had been an addled child named Aggie, in an awful barren west Kansas town called Weed. Chi shot down the man who hurt her, but it wasn't enough; the girl killed herself anyway, and something in Chi as well. Chi had been weeks getting out of her sorrow. Now she was taking to this Kelsey in something of the same way. Cord thought, *she is old enough to be the girl's mother*, and was startled and a little frightened. How had the time gotten away?

Cord felt a bit left out, and he thumped the gelding and rode up between the two women. Chi glanced at him curiously. "You did not tell one part," she said to Kelsey. "The part about the money?"

"Money?" Kelsey echoed artlessly.

"How much did you take out of that bank?"

"Don't know. We were riding hard, it was dark, he was drinking . . ." Kelsey kept her head down.

"*Hermana*," Chi said reproachfully.

"About twelve thousand," Kelsey admitted. "We rough-counted it before we bedded down."

"Give it over," Chi said.

The girl looked surprised. "I left it . . . with him."

"You trust your partner?"

"Do you?" the girl snapped.

"*Lo siento*," Chi murmured. She got another idea. "But you never meant to keep that appointment with Ryker in Casper. You had better ideas about that bank money."

Kelsey reined up. "You'd think about it, same as we did. But we gave the idea up. Couldn't see any sensible way around to do both, get the money and stay clear of him."

"Until you spotted us on your back-trail," Cord said.

"The only way we could run out on Ryker is if he was dead, and we don't know nothing about killing."

"But we do, right?" Cord said. "We could do your killing for you."

"Why sure," the girl said happily, oblivious to Cord's irony.

"We kill Ryker," Chi said, "and you get the money."

"We got to have it. We need a ticket out of this life, me and him."

"Twelve thousand dollars," Cord said. "That's one goddamned expensive ticket."

Kelsey gave him a coy shrewd look. "You can have half."

"Much obliged," Cord said solemnly.

"That's right," Chi said with disgust. "If we do your killing, you got to pay. Cord, what is our price for gunning down a U.S. marshal?"

But Cord had stopped listening. He was staring up the trail and seeing trouble. Off to the south maybe a mile across the flats there was a little settlement, Waltman by the map. Cord could see the vague shapes of the hamlet's three structures—a mercantile, a stockyard, and a barroom, most likely—and a few ranch houses scattered about a half mile out.

Several hundred yards ahead, as the trail skirted north of the little encampment, it threaded down through a brushy, sloped natural cut. At its foot, before the trail widened again, Cord saw light. He blinked, trying to will his eyes to make out detail, at the same time weighing the degree of danger against the disadvantages of instant flight.

"The train," Cord muttered, mostly to himself. It was the freight he had heard passing north of the trail a few hours earlier. The crew had spread the word all along the track by now, how the notorious Cord and Chi were worth government reward money, breathing or stiff. Who could guess how many bands of ham-assed farmers were roaming the countryside this minute, dreaming of glory in the service of order and decency, and more money in one night than they could make in three wet years in a row?

What this looked like was a roadblock. The point of light resolved into the flare of a pitch-soaked pine-knot torch. A buckboard was crossways in the road and four men stood alongside.

Damn them anyway, Cord thought. He was out of patience and too concerned for the horses to turn and run. But then it was decided, because behind them a raspy half scared voice said, "Freeze right there." Behind them were two men with old Henry .44 lever-action rifles.

"Do it," Cord said. "We don't need some dryland farmer's blood on our hands along with everything else."

The old man was about fifty, bare-headed and bald; the kid was in his early twenties, but as hairless as his pa, and slack-jawed to boot. Both wore faded coveralls. "Hands up," the old man said in his cracking tone.

"Goddamn, Daddy," the kid said. "It's them, sure as hell. Goddamn if we don't got 'em."

"Shut up, Tector." The old man jabbed his Henry at Cord. "I'll shoot you dead."

Jesus, Cord thought with cold panic, *the old fool is going to do it*. His leg muscles tensed as he readied to dive from the saddle. But then the old man waved the rifle and said, "Ride on down to that wagon, and keep 'em high all the time." Cord relaxed only relatively. There was nothing so dangerous as a weapon in the hands of a frightened amateur.

There was more of the same waiting at the wagon, another dirt-buster and his three drooling sons, each of them wide as a door. The father had the torch and the two older boys waved big old-fashioned single-action horse pistols. They stared at Cord and the two women as if this was the raciest sight in these parts since the tent show with the Egyptian dancers came through, two years ago next May.

"Gather in them guns, Tector," the old man ordered. He was puffing a mite in front of his friends.

"Hold up," Cord said, and tried a smile. He was temporizing. Running without their rifles was bad enough; if they lost their revolvers they were finished.

"We know you." Tector had a high whiny voice. "Yes we do." The three teen-aged boys nodded solemnly, their frayed straw hats bobbing in unison. "We got the word."

"And now we got you." The farmer at the head of the buckboard waved his torch. The two-horse team shied from the flame, and the tug chains rattled. "Two thousand on each of them is what the conductor said. That's..." He frowned, stared at his fingers. "That's plenty, even split six ways."

"Two ways is how it gets split," the old man on the horse snapped. "One share for each family, that's fair."

"Says you, Keets, you damned old fool."

"Shut up. You watch your boys, is what you do, watch your boys and shut up. Now, Tector, do as I say and get their goddamn guns."

Tector looked doubtful. Kelsey probably struck him as the least dangerous, because he sidled around and moved his horse up beside hers. Watching her face, he groped for the butt of her scabbarded Winchester. At the same time, Cord bent and jerked the torch from the farmer's hand, and the two horses reared in panic. Cord whirled and threw the flaming pine-knot at the man's three sons, jerking desperately on the reins at the same time, as the bay gelding had not been educated to the vagaries of fire. One of the horse pistols went off and a juvenile voice screamed, "You shot me in the goddamned foot!"

Chi yanked the Henry away from old man Keets. Kelsey

pulled her revolver and whipped it across Tector's face. Blood flecked from his cheek and Tector fell out of the saddle without a whimper.

"Go!" Cord hollered and they did, at a low flat-out run. Behind them another of the farm boys fired his pistol, but by then they were out of the old gun's range, which was about a foot and a half.

Cord called a halt within a mile, soon as they were over a rise and out of sight. That crew had other things on their minds besides chase now, and they had to save the horses at all costs.

Chi pulled up beside Cord and began to laugh. "Yeah," Cord breathed, seeing the tangle of confused and damaged farmers, and began to laugh with her. Kelsey sat her horse to one side, watching them as if the tension of the encounter had driven them crazy.

Cord drew a breath and got himself stopped. It was not so much funny as pointless, which was something like the same thing. You could survive a lifetime of facing up to fast guns and tenacious lawmen, to get your ass blown off by a cluster of panicky hayseeds armed with rusty museum pieces. There was never going to be a smart way to die, but goddamn what a stupid way that would have been— and it could have happened, almost did.

"Stop that," Kelsey said sharply.

Chi checked her laughing. "Are you afraid?"

"I was. I'm not now."

"Good." Chi smiled at Cord. *Mi hermana.*

"Sure," Cord said. "She did fine." He studied the sky. "Let's find a rock to crawl under. I got a feeling tomorrow is going to be a long day."

Chapter Fourteen

CORD FELT THE PRESSURE OF A HAND ON HIS shoulder and opened his eyes to look up into Chi's face. His first groggy thought was about how fine it would be to awaken every morning to that touch, that sight—and then he remembered where he was, and why.

"What?" he muttered.

"Take a look."

Cord felt the warmth of her hand through his clothing. There was a tiny delta of wrinkles in the corner of each of her eyes; Cord had never noticed them before. Her olive skin was smooth over her high handsome cheekbones, and her thin lips were parted a bit to show straight ivory teeth.

She shook her head very slightly and took her hand away. Cord kicked the saddle blanket off and stood, unsteady for a moment, rubbing the sleep from his eyes with the side of his fist. He never used to sleep so soundly on the trail, Cord thought. But she had been on watch...

They were holed up in a little nest of rocks, a couple of hundred yards above the trail up one of the creek draws that cut the foothills of the southern leg of the Big Horn Mountains. The road had forked a half dozen miles back, Bridger's branch cutting north toward the Big Horn Basin while Price Hunt's trail dipped down toward Atlantic City and South Pass. Kelsey turned them to the right at the fork, though she stayed cagey about exactly where they were supposed to be heading. She lay in the shelter of a boulder, curled up with her knees drawn to her chin, sucking at a knuckle in her sleep.

Stars still blinked in the direction of the mountains, but the eastern sky was beginning to lighten. Cord pulled on his boots and followed Chi, feeling stiff and still a trifle muddle-headed, with no coffee this morning either. He fished out his pouch, then decided he did not want a smoke badly enough to take the trouble to roll one. Chi led him up the gravel bed of a tiny spring-fed trickle to a shelf of rock, both of them staying low.

"There." Chi handed Cord his spyglass. From the rock shelf he could see about a mile down the swale cradling the main leg of the trail. A sliver of sun glared into his eyes at the horizon line. Cord squinted into the brightness.

Ten minutes away, Ryker and company were coming up the swale. Ryker was leaned forward in the saddle with his hands crossed on the forks, so his high-crowned hat was aimed at them like a huge bullet. The three Payne boys were drowsing horseback, but Bernard Pearl was bright-eyed and looking nervously around.

Mr. Earl was crouched on his haunches in the road, staring into the dirt like some old Roman inspecting the entrails of a sacrificed goat. The ridiculous-looking Indian said something over his shoulder to Ryker, then pointed directly at Cord and Chi.

They were behind cover and there was no way he could see them, but still it was eerie. "One thing we can't do is hole up and hope they ride past," Cord muttered. "That Indian is too uncanny. He'd follow our track up here like it was a city sidewalk."

"Let him." It was Kelsey, crawled up behind them.

"Get back," Cord ordered.

"We can take them," she insisted. "Finish them off here and now."

"Is that what *we* can do?" Cord said. At this early hour he was easily irritated.

"Cord!" Chi said.

Cord scowled and felt like a cranky old coot who had no patience for nonsense before coffee. "Let's just see to the horses," he grumbled, and edged back from the lookout.

"So we are running out again," Kelsey pressed.

"That is right, girl, and every minute we waste comes off our head start."

Chi did not argue. She knew the alternatives as well as he. This draw closed out somewhere above; if they stayed put they would play into Ryker's plan to bottle them and wait until they got hungry enough to eat dirt. Even if Cord and Chi could provoke the fight, they were still outgunned, outnumbered, and pinned down.

Kelsey watched the two of them check their saddles. "Don't dawdle, girl," Cord snapped like a stern father. Kelsey scrambled to where she'd left her tack and began saddling her mount.

"They are going to spot us soon as we come out of this draw," Cord said. "Maybe sooner, and from damned close. When we hit the main trail, get your head down and ride."

Cord led them down the draw toward the open swale of the main trail. A couple miles north, the way they were heading, it narrowed as it entered the steeper mountain cuts. There was the first goal.

They edged around a layered shale outcrop, and there they were, Ryker and his gang, barely two hundred yards back, clustered behind the bronze-chested Mr. Earl. Cord registered two impressions: the surprise on Ryker's face, and the shrewd appraising gaze of Mr. Earl, like a predator assessing its prey. The low sun made his tinted eyeglasses sparkle like rubies.

Then Cord was raking the bay and the big animal responded, driving hard into a low-ground-drumming run. Within seconds gunfire erupted behind them. Cord risked a look back: Chi and Kelsey were hard on his trail, and beyond them Cord got a glimpse of Ryker's men sighting rifles. Ryker shouted and threw up a hand, but one of the Payne cousins broke loose and came after them anyway at a loping gallop.

Chi's mare lurched as its left forefoot caught a rabbit hole. The horse caught itself, staggered, and went down and over in a long rolling fall, legs kicking madly. Horse and rider disappeared for a moment in a chalky cloud of alkaline dust before Chi rolled clear.

Cord jerked back, setting up his bay in the dust, the horse spinning before responding to spurs, and plunging back the way they had come. Chi made her knees before Cord reached her, shaky but nothing broken. The mare was also whole and on its feet now, but Chi remained on hands and knees, her head hanging down. Cord drew his Colt and fired two shots in Ryker's direction without aiming, then sprang to the ground, grabbed Chi by the arm.

She looked up at him dimly.

"Goddamn it. Get up!"

The Payne cousin with heroic notions was fifty yards away and closing hard and fast. Ryker hollered behind him.

The Payne cousin fired his rifle one-handed and the slug plowed into the ground a yard to one side. Cord jerked Chi to her feet, dragged her to the mare, gathered up the reins, and got her left foot in the stirrup.

The Payne boy levered the Winchester, flipping it by the handle. The hooves of his horse pounded loudly on the alkali as he raised to fire again. Cord let go of Chi and aimed the Colt with both hands, standing splayed-legged and steady.

But the rifle shot came from behind him, and the Payne boy jerked and hunched awkwardly over his horse's neck. He swayed one way and then the other as the horse plunged toward Cord, and then he came out of the saddle, flipped loose-limbed in the dirt, and rolled to a stop almost at Cord's feet. Cord danced back as the man's heart pumped a last great fountain through the hole in his chest. Blood bubbled in the dirt.

Cord grabbed up the Winchester, then boosted Chi into the saddle, grabbed up the reins, and pressed them into her hands. Pearl and the other two were firing all around them. Cord vaulted on the bay and whacked the rump of Chi's mare with the butt of the rifle. The mare jumped forward and Chi came around. Cord raced after her and Kelsey swung around to join them, her Winchester across her saddle. They raced up the narrowing cut, out of range and then around a bend and out of Ryker's sight.

Cord reined up and they waited a couple of minutes. Ryker did not follow. He was holding, sticking to his plan. Probably standing over the Payne boy's corpse right now, telling the other two cousins that here was what happened when you did not follow orders, went off half-cocked . . .

"Everyone okay?" But then Cord saw the smear of blood on Chi's handsome face.

"*Nada*," Chi said angrily. She pushed back her sombrero and wiped at her temple with the edge of her serape. There wasn't much blood, only a scratch that Cord could see. "Damn those pig bastards." She hated being the one who fell, even if it was not her fault. At least she was not really hurt; Cord felt deep relief.

Kelsey was not doing as well. She was trembling so violently she could not fit her rifle into its scabbard. Chi shook cobwebs out of her head and sidled her mare next to Kelsey. Chi took the rifle and seated it in the sheath, then held the girl's hand. Kelsey began to sob.

"For Christ's sake," Cord muttered.

"You hold your tongue, Cord!" Chi snapped.

"No time for this," Cord said.

Kelsey snuffled and wiped her nose on the back of her hand. "I'm good enough."

"She killed a man," Chi said. "You think about your first time."

Or the last time, Cord thought. The girl was confronting something new here, something always new and never pleasant.

Chi stroked Kelsey's hand. "*Mi hermana*," she murmured. Chi released Kelsey's hand, turned her horse, and squared herself in the saddle.

"All right, Mr. Cord," she said. "The ladies are ready to ride."

Chapter Fifteen

"WE ARE GOING NORTH," KELSEY SAID.

Cord sat his horse and studied her. "No, we're not," he said evenly.

Kelsey looked at him, perplexed and childlike. She had calmed herself, come to terms for now with the killing of Ryker's man. They were ten miles further on now, at a crossroads amid the piney forested slopes up Bridger Creek into the boot of the Big Horn range. The morning sun was high in the sky.

"We are not going anywhere, *hija*," Chi explained. "Not until you tell us what we will find at the end of trail."

The dead Payne boy's Winchester was lashed on behind Cord's saddle. He retied the knots, watching the girl.

"There is a place called Thermopolis," Kelsey said.

"Grecos?" Chi wondered. "A hot city of Greeks."

"What are you talking about?" Cord stared at her.

"'Thermopolis,'" Chi said. "In Greek that means a hot city."

Cord could not have been more mystified had *she* been speaking Greek. "How do you know that?"

"My father sent me to convent school, in Mexico City, when I was a *muchacha* and didn't know any better."

"I never knew that."

"Lots you don't know, Mr. Cord," Chi said smugly.

"That's for damned sure," Cord muttered.

"Tell me about this hot city," Chi said to Kelsey.

"There's springs there. Sulphur water, pouring out of the rocks day and night. You can smell it a mile away, like a million rotten eggs."

"And why do we go there?"

"My partner is waiting. That's the place we're supposed to meet in case of trouble, like I told you about. Fifty miles—we can make it by nightfall."

"If we do," Cord said, "the horses are done. They will be down for days."

"Don't matter. There is no farther to go. That is the end, one way or the other."

Killing a man had put steel in her spine. It worked that way with some people.

"Half dozen years back," Kelsey continued, "an old outlaw named Buskirk rode in and bought the springs from the Arapaho for two hundred dollars cash money."

"What for?"

"He turned it into a spa."

"A what?" Cord was bewildered: Chi speaking Greek, and now this. . . .

"He built a hotel and a bathhouse. Folk come from all over, Baltimore, places like that, to soak in that sulphur water and drink it with their suppers."

"Why?"

"How would I know?" Kelsey said impatiently. "But they pay money for it, and Buskirk must figure that's better than a sharp kick in the ass. Anyway, my partner knows him from the old days, and as those eastern folks don't arrive until the snow is clear gone from the passes, we made an arrangement." Kelsey jerked her horse toward the right-hand road. "We are wasting time."

"Looks like it," Chi said laconically. She pointed back the way they'd come.

And there they were, Ryker and his bully boys, coming into sight where the trail snaked up the Bridger Creek drainage, two and a half, three miles back.

"Who are those boys with him?" Cord asked. The way this was heading, it was best to have all the puzzle pieces laid out before him.

"Deputies." Kelsey laughed humorlessly. "Ryker swore them in not long after he came to Wyoming. Caught them rustling cows through Hole-in-the-Wall and offered them a deal. Probably told them it was a safer way to go, but it wasn't, not for one of them anyway." Her laugh was too shrill. A kid trying to show how tough she could be, Cord thought, and God bless her.

"The one I killed was Boone," Kelsey said. "Bye, bye, Boone." She brought herself up short. "Cousins named Payne, just folks with guns. Like us."

"You'd best hope you are wrong, girl." Cord took a last look, then spun his bay. "Let's move."

A few minutes later he came up beside Chi, in the lead. "How do you like being on the run again?"

"Not so much," Chi said. "Let's make sure it doesn't happen again."

"No more," Cord agreed. "Not after this."

Chapter Sixteen

"**H**OW MUCH FURTHER?" CORD ASKED.
"Use your nose, *querido*," Chi suggested.

At first Cord scented only musty night and trail dust. It was two hours past full dark; the trip had taken longer than they'd reckoned. As they climbed toward the headwaters of Bridger Creek, the creek became a little rill between steep-sloped banks. Patches of old corn snow covered shaded sections of the trail, and the quarter mile on either side of the pass was drifted three feet deep in places, the snow stiff and crusty. The horses' hooves cut through the frozen top and the going became aggravatingly slow. By the time they came down the far side and cut the South Fork of the Kirby, most of the daytime was lost. Twilight edged toward night as they rode out onto the enormous plain of the Big Horn Basin.

The sun splashed streaks of red and yellow and purple. The moon came up within minutes, peering between coagulating slathers of gray cloud. A gusty breeze, driving chill air down from the eastern slope of the Continental Divide, a hundred miles toward the lost sunset, blew in their faces and a thunderstorm swept through the Basin ahead of them. They rode in darkness through the sweetish stink of wet sage, on to Big Horn River.

The clouds closed in as they turned upriver and it began to drizzle. Heads down, they rode south another five miles, toward what the map called Wedding of the Waters, where the river climbed and narrowed into the impassable Wind River Canyon. Cord drew another deep breath through his nose and caught a faint acrid chemical whiff. "About time," he muttered. He led them up toward a little ridge. The sharp stink of the sulphur springs grew more pungent and the roar of the water became louder, too quickly to be the canyon rapids.

"We made it," Kelsey called through the rain. "Over that last rise."

"Wonderful." Cord was light-headed from lack of sleep and the tension of being run like a coyote caught killing sheep. Rainwater dribbled from his hat brim and down inside his shirt. He'd been holding his neck muscles tight; he rolled his shoulders and shook out his arms. One last rise.

This was no sane occupation for a grown man. How long had he been riding into these places in the night, too weary to worry about who was waiting? But no one forced you to sit down at the table, so there was no point grousing about the cards you got dealt. One thing, though: Once they were out of this mess there was going to be some serious rethinking. For him and Chi. For them.

"There she sits."

Cord looked up, startled by Kelsey's voice close beside him. Thermopolis had snuck up on him.

They were on the rim of a semicircle of hillside cradling

a half bowl of bench several hundred feet across. It opened to the west, where it was cut abruptly by the fifty-foot-deep river gorge. The east slope of the bowl was a series of six terrace steps, and from this porous volcanic rock the hot sulphur water gushed. This was no trickle spring, but a scalding, cascading waterfall that erupted full-blown out of nowhere, as much water as in a good-sized river. Slimy yellow sulphur deposits frosted the terraces in vast frozen undulating sheets and graceful swirls.

The terraces were maybe fifty yards wide, and fell about the same distance from the top stair step to where the 135-degree water plunged in long sheets over the lip of the canyon to the chill snow-packed flow of Big Horn River. Mushrooming clouds of steam billowed up into the night, and the rain hissed like a field of grasshoppers as it slanted into the hot terraces. Cord had never seen any landscape as alien or surreal, even up in Yellowstone Park or Colter's Hell; something unworldly was happening here, something that drew him into deep and vaguely uncomfortable timelessness. And that damned smell, thick enough to gag a hog...

"Follow me," Kelsey said happily. The trail switchbacked down the north face of the bowl to its bottom, where a plank walkway crossed the bottom terrace. The tired gelding snorted and rolled its eyes, spooked by the stink and the rolling clouds of obscuring steam. Cord kept the reins taut and his own eyes straight ahead; he liked this no better than the horse. To the right, as they reached the end of the planks, a narrow suspension bridge swayed above the river canyon in the stiff breeze. An aversion to heights had dogged Cord since he was a boy, and the notion of crossing the narrow vertiginous span, swinging wide as the pendulum in a grandfather clock, made his guts lurch.

This Buskirk character had made himself a nice enough

little nest in which to pass his last years. At the upriver end, an aqueduct ran down along the side of the terraces to a large pavilion, the bathhouse. At each shelf a sluice gate admitted the spring water. None was open now, and the pine-tarred wooden flume was empty save for a trickle of rainwater. Behind the bathhouse there was a small barn with an attached corral.

The hotel building on the other side of the wagon track running up from the suspension bridge was three stories high, nothing fancy but sturdy enough. A roof to keep out the rain and a fire at least, maybe even some coffee, thought Cord. Coffee would be fine. At first it looked dark as the cavernous bathhouse, but as they came off the boardwalk Cord caught the glimmer of a lantern behind a window next to the front door. Kelsey hollered, "Hello, the hotel!" No one answered. "Mr. Buskirk—you in there, old man?"

"Let's get out of this damned rain," Chi muttered. Kelsey swung down and stomped up on the porch. The front door opened and lantern light silhouetted the figure of a man with thick flowering whiskers.

"That you, girl?" The old man stepped out and raised the lantern. "Who is that with you? Never mind. Come in here."

Chi watched slump-shouldered from the saddle, and Cord, back to thinking coffee, realized suddenly that she was as tired as he was. Over the years he had come to think of her stamina as infinite; there were times, more than one, when there were guns behind them and they'd been forced to spend most of three or four days in the saddle. He would turn mush-minded with fatigue, while she sat straight and graceful and stoic through rain, dust, and a butt-busting eternity of riding.

"You go on." Cord leaned over, took her reins, and

flipped them forward over the mare's head. "I'll see to the animals."

She smiled wearily. "You doing all right, *querido*?" But she did not protest. *"Gracias."* She pulled the Waltman farmer's Henry rifle from her scabbard and slid out of the saddle.

"What do you think?" Cord blustered. "Sure I'm all right." He was not accustomed to her going soft on him. But then he had maybe saved her life that day, and she was not accustomed to that. Both of them were acting out of nature, but nothing wrong with that either. That damned Boone Payne, firing his rifle and trying to ride them down . . . Cord gathered up the reins of Kelsey's horse and rode around along the wagon track.

Two other animals were stalled inside the small livery barn. They snorted when Cord flung open the door, as if they had not seen much company through the winter. Cord found a lantern on a peg inside the door jamb and a dry lucifer inside his coat pocket. A dozen laying hens were roosting toward the back part of the barn and the air was thick with the sweet smell of slightly fermented hay. The horses' eyes were wild and spooky in the flickering light of the coal-oil wick. Cord flopped up a stirrup and undid each cinch, dragged the saddles off and rested each on the pole rack, working mechanically and ignoring the ache in his shoulders and lower back. With each horse in a stall, he climbed the ladder to the overhead hay loft and pitched down a few forkfuls, breathing the dust and grunting. Below again, he raised the lantern and checked once more, aware he was tired enough to forget little things if he did not take care. But everything appeared satisfactory, and he walked around through the rain to the front of the hotel.

The shingle over the porch's canopy read "THERMOPOLIS HOUSE." The front room, a sort of lounge, was decorated in a fantastic Western style for the diversion of the summer guests from back east. Above the writing desk were mounted the heads of two deer and a giant sorrowful moose; a fat varnished cutthroat trout on a platter-shaped board hung near the door. The chandelier was a refinished buggy wheel, and here and there were potted cacti. The substantial chairs and couches were built of grainy dark wood and covered with a thick coat of shellac that reflected the gleam of brass cuspidors.

Inside the six-foot firebox of a big stone-masonry fireplace, a newly built fire was crackling and sending flames up into the flue. Opposite, an archway opened into a dim dining room where neatly set wooden tables awaited diners. In front of a pigeonhole rack in the corner, a big leather-bound register book faced out on the counter of the check-in desk, and next to it a stairway climbed to the rooms on the upper floors.

The most striking piece of woodworking in the place was the ornate bar fronting the other corner. The Long Bar, they called it. It was the type that was shipped around the Horn to California in gold rush days. When the boom was over, a lot of these old bars made their way inland by rail, shipped in numbered sections. This one was carved dark oak with a brilliant brass rail, topped with a single plank three inches thick, with an inlaid gutter. Neat rows of bottles and precise pyramids of glasses sat before a polished mirror on the back shelf. Everything was orderly and in good repair; here was the house of a person who took care.

The ambient rotten-egg smell was inside too, but Cord scented a richer aroma cutting through it. "Would that be coffee?"

The whiskered man appeared out of the dining room's dimness, carrying his lantern and pewter pot. He shined the light in Cord's face as if searching for an honest man. "I know you," he declared. The old man had a high voice and a broad accent with a residue of Scotch-Irish left in it. "Never mind that," he said. "Have your coffee, son."

Buskirk set the lantern on the bar and blew it out, found a cup and poured for Cord. The coffee was hot and thick and strong, the way Cord made it himself. Chi sprawled in one of the heavy chairs, her eyes half closed and her cup ignored in her hands. She spotted Cord and smiled weakly. Kelsey leaned against the front desk taking quick shallow sips of the dark brew and looking more impatient than tired.

The old man tapped Cord on the shoulder. He splashed a dollop of bourbon into Cord's coffee. Cord smiled weakly. The coffee and whiskey tasted like heaven.

Buskirk was looking him over again. The one-time outlaw was somewhere beyond fifty, a head shorter than Cord, wiry except for a hint of gut over the waistband of his baggy corduroy britches, which were held up by suspenders over a plaid woolen shirt. His thin hair bristled like straw around a bald circle on the crown of his pate, and his black-flecked gray whiskers covered his collar. The dozen or so teeth he had left were long and yellow-brown.

"You need another." Buskirk pointed to Cord's cup, took it behind the bar, and refilled it with equal parts of coffee and bourbon. Kelsey stood at the front window staring into the rain and darkness, and Chi had put her cup down and looked to be dozing. A pitch-knot exploded and sparks leaped up the chimney. Chi stirred and murmured something in Spanish.

Buskirk gave Cord his cup, then stood back and went on staring at him. "I know you," he said again.

"Is that right?" Cord drank.

"You're Elegant John Odum out of Burns, Oregon."

This jasper was serving up wonderful coffee laced with

whiskey, and his hotel was warm and clean and dry. "Whatever you say," Cord told him.

Buskirk laughed, showing his colorful teeth. "You ain't Elegant John Odum. Nothing elegant about you."

At the window, Kelsey said, "Where is he, Mr. Buskirk?"

Buskirk ignored her. "But I do know you, son, just the same, so you listen up. You too, lady." Chi opened her eyes and turned her head a little.

"I've been a hooligan and a roughneck in my day," Buskirk said. "I have been a scapegrace and a scalawag, no denying it. I ain't ashamed..." Buskirk grinned shrewdly. "I've made my peace with the Lord."

"Good for you."

"I know which way the trail runs, Mr. Cord."

The old man was a trifle ringy, Cord decided, but likely not clear crazy.

"So here is the drill: you have the hospitality of my house, but you got to promise that you ain't going to bust things up. This is my place."

Nothing crazy about that. Old Man Buskirk had found a hutch where he could live out his last days in serenity, catering to fools in the summer and taking their money legally, hunkering down in warmth and comfort and isolation through the dark months. *This is where I live*, the old man was saying. *Do not tread on my toes, and do not screw up this good deal of mine*.

"How do you stand the stink?"

"You get used to it, son. Get used to most anything, when you're old as me. I go down to Casper, Cheyenne, where all them people are tight up together—I can smell them all right. That is what I call a stink."

"Please, Mr. Buskirk." Kelsey spoke softly but urgently. "Where is he?"

Buskirk stared at her absently, as if he wasn't sure whom she was talking about. He blinked. "Patrolling. Getting the lay of the land. Taking precautions." Before Cord could cipher where this new tack headed, Buskirk nodded over his shoulder and said, "There he be."

Boot heels rapped on the porch floor boards and lantern light flickered in the window then winked out. The door opened and a young man entered. A slouch hat was pulled low over his face against the rain, the brim bent down.

Kelsey went to him and put her hand on his arm. The young man peered at her from under the hat brim. He wore a shapeless rubberized poncho. He pulled away from her and went to the fire, stood with his back to all of them, as if unaware, or reluctant to acknowledge, that he was not alone. He shook the loose folds of the poncho and droplets of water sizzled. He slapped his hat against his thigh, replaced it atop thinning sandy hair, and held his hands out to the warmth of crackling flames.

But then his shoulders hunched and tensed, as if he had resolved to delay inevitable confrontation no longer. The young man turned, and he was not so young, with a worn drawn gaunt face that testified to some rough worrisome times since Cord and Chi had seen him last.

Chi sat up straight in the chair and shot Cord a look. But Cord had recognized him too: the missing piece in this jigsaw puzzle. This hollow-cheeked man was the same boy who had run them down for Enos Ryker the first time, five years ago near Grand Island, Nebraska.

Kelsey's partner was Kyle Greer.

Chapter Seventeen

CORD SAT LIKE A GENTLEMAN BEFORE THE FIRE in one of the armchairs, sipping his third cup of coffee and bourbon. "Good," he murmured.

"You bet your ass, son." Buskirk showed him the bottle. "Private stock, lookee here."

Sure enough, the label featured a lithographic rendering of sulphur terraces, steam rising into the sunshine, and beneath:

OLD VICKSBURG BOURBON WHISKEY

Bottled from Special Reserves
For the Express Enjoyment of the Clients,
Thermopolis House,
Abraham Buskirk, Prop.

"Abraham?" Cord asked lazily.

"Don't be making fun, sonny. The *turistas* think they are being treated mighty special, and they will pay extra to feel like big shots. Money in the bank for me." He gave Cord a shrewd look. "Big city bank, with triple-thick rock walls, time-lock vaults, and Pinkerton guards. A bank where a feller like you came in, they'd shoot you on looks alone. Ain't one of those crackerboxes you and the lady are used to, so don't be getting ideas."

"You do go on, *viejo*," Chi said sleepily.

"Hell yes I do," Buskirk exclaimed. "Ain't talked to no one in three months, except for Tommy Two-Head and his son Buck Knife, come calling every other Sunday night to drink my whiskey and cheat at pinochle, and most all they speak is Arapaho."

Cord sat with his drink and a cigarette, only his second of the long day, out of his wet coat, his britches steaming and mostly dry, content as a cat for right now. Cord had never been in a place quite like this Thermopolis House. He'd heard of such resort spas springing up here and there in the years since the northwestern corner of the Territory had been turned into a National Park. The West was becoming increasingly more like a circus: come and see the great wilderness, from a comfortable box seat. Parks and hostelries, glib-talking guides and lots of black-powder smoke and blank cartridges. It was as if Buffalo Bill's Wild West had become the world, so the real thing must imitate the show. The notion did not make Cord glum as it once might have, merely thoughtful. And here was Abraham Buskirk, selling magic water that sluiced the aches and pains away, and telling somewhat true tales of his desperado days. Cord smiled: good for the old thief. He had discovered the secret of evading death by gun shot or a lifetime wasting in jail: become an innkeeper.

Chi sat on the other side of the fireplace. Her serape

hung with his coat over the hearth, and she looked fine and womanly in her wool shirt and dark leather britches and long intricate braids. In contrast, Kelsey looked like a boy waiting to grow up. She sipped black coffee at the desk, in canvas farmer pants held aloft by braces over a dirty cotton union suit. She had narrow shoulders and tiny breasts, sexless as a child's.

Buskirk stood behind the bar, the proper host. "There is one thing," he announced.

Cord sighed and turned his head.

"I got me an arrangement with Missy here and her beau, but you two has got to pay the freight. Regular rates, one night in advance."

"How much?" Cord said wearily. He expected to be gouged. Buskirk knew who they were, maybe why they were on the run and hunkering in. The old man might have been shooting with damp powder, but he was not dumb.

Buskirk gave the ceiling a shrewd look, as if he were ciphering columns of figures in his head. "Ten dollars," he announced. "Per night, each person. Meals included, whiskey extra, and you two have already run up a two-dollar tab in that department."

"Here, *viejo*." Chi fished bills from the pocket of her britches, peeled off a hundred.

Buskirk frowned at the banknote. "I'll fetch your change."

"Better wait until we check out," Chi suggested. "My partner can tote up some kind of bar bill."

"Just so he don't wreck anything." The hundred-dollar note found a home in Buskirk's shirt pocket.

Nothing was going to be wrecked. There were times when Cord needed a snootful the night before some showdown, but this was not one.

Chi turned abruptly in her chair. Kyle Greer came out of the shadows on the staircase into the edge of the firelight near the bottom. He held a sawed-off shotgun by its grip, barrels pointed at the floor.

Time was not his friend. The boy Cord had run into five years earlier could not be older than twenty-five or -six now, but Kyle Greer was aged by something timeless, and likely painful. His sandy hair was streaked with dirty gray and thin enough to show freckled scalp beneath. His 'mustache wanted trimming, and its bushy line emphasized the gauntness of his concave cheeks and the hollow depths of his eye sockets. He looked like he slept badly and had nightmares.

He wore gabardine trousers and a faded patched shirt buttoned to the neck. He held his hat in one hand, toting it around as if he were afraid it might be stolen. Cord kept an eye on the shotgun in the other.

Greer had come in out of the rain and stared at them, as if trying to decide if it might be possible to pretend not to know who they were. He looked at Kelsey and snapped, "What goes on?" and, before she could answer, said, "Never mind," in a curiously neutral tone. He had pushed past and gone upstairs without another look. That was maybe ten minutes ago.

Now he stood on the bottom step, mostly giving Cord the willies. There was something not right with this boy. Cord had been hoping that Kelsey's partner would be an extra gun on their side, but now he wondered if Greer was going to make the trouble worse. He knew them all right, no amount of squirrelly twitching was going to change that.

"Nice gun, boy," Cord said. He wondered if it was loaded. "Sawed-off, like Ryker's. Is he your hero, boy? You want to be like him when you get grown?"

Greer looked at him, curiously untouched by the needling, as if he had heard the sound of someone talking but could not make out the words. Kelsey went to him and took his arm near the biceps in both her hands. He looked at her. "They are not supposed to be here." His tone was more perplexed than accusatory.

"Might as well set down the scattergun, Kyle," Buskirk said matter-of-factly. "You don't need it just yet."

"Like hell I don't," Greer said in his flat mechanical voice.

Buskirk came around the bar and stalked up to Greer. He clapped his hands sharply twice, an inch away from Greer's nose. "Goddammit, boy, wake up."

Greer blinked and took a deep breath, looked around the room again as if he expected to see some subtle transmutation in the nature of things. Buskirk carefully lifted the shotgun out of his hands and stashed it behind the front desk's counter. Kelsey led Greer over to the bar and leaned him against it. With her he was at ease.

"He ain't twenty-four carat," Buskirk said to Cord. "Ain't been since he teamed with Ryker. They make a hell of a pair, both of them crazy as seven Swedes."

"They are going to help us, Kyle." At the bar, Kelsey was talking to Greer in a low voice. "Maybe kill Ryker for us, let us take the money..."

"Which money was that?" Chi asked sharply.

"Please," Kelsey pleaded, not for the money but for some little help with the job of humoring Kyle Greer.

"Jesus," Cord breathed. The kid really was crazy, not addled like old Buskirk but genuinely. Generally speaking, the insane made Cord nervous. "Goddammit, that boy is worse than useless. We're going to have to care for him like a baby. He's been like this for five years?"

"Not so bad as he is now," Buskirk said. "He started drifting after that run-in with you folks."

"What do you know, *viejo*?" Chi demanded.

"I know this," Buskirk said mildly. "I know what happened after you left Ryker tied to a tree buck-naked."

Buskirk looked shrewdly at Chi and his eyes brightened. He slapped his knee in self-appreciation. "The boy here told me how he cut him down. I laughed," Buskirk said. "Laughed right at him next time I was in Casper. He had to take it. I know things he don't want known, so I don't worry about Ryker. If he kills you, he won't get so mad he comes after me for letting you hole up."

"Bet you sleep easy," Cord said.

"Damned straight. Here is the rest: that time five years back, Ryker made the boy here steal him some clothes off a farmhouse washline in the middle of the night. Then Ryker gave Kyle a choice."

Greer had retreated back into some hideout on the far side of his mind. He stared at the floor.

"Kyle could spend the rest of his days behind bars," Buskirk said, "or he could do whatever damned thing Ryker told him."

"Bad as jail," Chi said.

"Sure, but the kid didn't know that—not until it drove him batshit—and then he didn't hardly know his name." Buskirk cackled.

"What did Ryker tell him to do?"

"Dirty things," Kelsey blurted. "Men got shot in the back." She took a step forward. "You'd do the same. You'd kill to stay out of jail."

Cord shook his head sadly.

"I didn't have to be part of this," Kelsey said, "but I did it. I would do anything for Kyle." She went on quickly. "Two years back he rode into Basin. I was sixteen and hated the idea of spilling my life like wash water. I watched my father try to run fifty cows on a dry-land section and drink himself to death at the same time, and my mother watching him. He was all the time grabbing at me. He'd whale me with his belt." Kelsey shuddered.

"Hermana." Chi looked entranced and touched by the story.

"Anyway," Kelsey said briskly. "Kyle rode through town and I saw him coming out of a saloon. We started talking..." She had gone coy. "We got on all right, and I talked him into taking me with him. Kyle never had no experience except with sporting women, and I never had no man. So it was like starting fresh for both of us."

No one spoke, which seemed to bother the girl, as if she expected a response, like reassurance. "I thought I could change him if I loved him hard." Kelsey went to Kyle Greer and turned. "Maybe I can," she said, like a dare.

Kyle Greer came to life, unglued himself from the bar, and straightened. He looked at each of them, ending with Kelsey. There is a boy with a short attention span, Cord thought. Greer yawned elaborately, crooked and straightened both arms. "We'd better catch some shut-eye," he said. Kelsey took his hand and led him up the stairs.

Chi stood. "What room are they in?" she asked Buskirk. "I don't want to walk in on the middle of any of *that.*"

"Take the one at the end of the corridor, two flights up," Buskirk suggested. "Finest suite in the house, little lady."

Chi was too tired to trade any more wisecracks. She waved vaguely at Cord and went after Greer and the girl.

Cord got up and put his cup on the bar. Buskirk refilled it without asking, but went easy on the bourbon this time. Last one tonight, Cord decided.

"What say?" Buskirk sounded in the mood for conversation.

Cord shook his head meaninglessly. Men would die the next morning, and no point in riding it into the ground.

Buskirk cleared his throat. "I got to go up to the Indian

camp tomorrow. Last I heard they was west of Kirby. Hope they ain't moved since."

Buskirk picked up Cord's cup and inhaled with gusto. "My but that smells like sweet dreams." He shook his head. "Me and Buck Knife, who is the chief now that his pa Tommy Two-Head is retired, we got to sign a contract for the coming tourist season. His Arapaho are my meat hunters, bring me buffalo from up near the Park. Tougher than a boot, but them dudes cannot get enough."

Buskirk stared into the cup. "What I'm saying is, I am out of this fight. I am gone before sunup."

"It's always good to be horseback when the sun appears," Cord agreed.

"The thing is, I am too old for this." He poked a finger at Cord. "You remember, no busting up my place. This resort spa is the home I never had."

Cord finished his drink. "You got any guns, old man?"

Buskirk gave Cord his shrewd speculative look. "Sure," he said. "You got any plans?"

Chapter Eighteen

CORD LAY IN THE CHILL DARKNESS OF A SEC-ond floor bedroom, smoking a ramshackle cigarette he had built himself, and thinking—could not stop himself—thinking how lucky he was. Not trapped like Kelsey, not off in never-never land like Kyle Greer. Soon as this mess was over he was heading for his first chance at land of his own, and Chi was even making odd noises like she could think of nothing better. If that wasn't luck...

He'd had luck much of his life, Cord decided. He'd been strong enough to survive the sort of searching that had addled Kyle Greer, and strength was a sort of luck: the luck of being born with quick hands and good intuition.

Kyle Greer had become confused and his confusion had to trap him, in a real prison or the one in his head. Kelsey had made a bad trade, her abusive father for Greer. She'd be caring for the boy like he was her child, all the rest of her life. He and Chi had avoided such traps, and now was the time to get out. Cord thanked his stars.

But there was this Ryker business . . .

Knuckles rapped on the door. Cord stubbed out his cigarette in a dish beside the lantern on the night table and threw back the quilt. He padded across the dark room in his union suit, thinking pleasurably that it was Chi.

It was Kelsey.

"What?" Cord said, disconcerted and sounding cross.

Kelsey ducked under his arm. Cord shut the door and leaned against it. A woman coming in the night could be low adventure, but he was in no mood for this one. He felt halfway naked and more than a little stupid, standing in his union suit, but Kelsey did not seem to notice.

"You'll do it, won't you."

Cord peered at her. "Do what?"

"What you promised."

"Nobody made any promises . . . promised what?"

Kelsey went to the window. Beyond her the terraces steamed white shadows above the dark hulk of the bath-house. "Sometimes he gets better," she said. "That bank job in Casper, he pulled it off without hearing voices or seeing monsters. Ryker can scare him gentle sometimes. Kyle still ain't right, but he can see to business, like his brains are unhooked but his flywheel is still spinning. Do you know what I mean?"

"No," Cord said. He wanted this girl out of his room.

"But when he has to do Ryker's dirty work, Kyle goes back into a state. It takes longer each time before I can bring him back, and he always stops short of getting to where he was before. So I know what will happen, next job or the one after that, Kyle'll be gone for good, and useless."

For Cord's money the boy was already useless.

"Ryker will kill him soon as that happens—unless we kill Ryker first."

"Who is going to do the deed?"

"I love that benighted boy, Mr. Cord." She drew breath, steeling herself for what came next. "I'll show you how much."

Kelsey flopped the suspenders off her shoulders and pulled the top of her union suit over her head, so quickly Cord could do nothing except stand there with his mouth open. She came and put her arms around his neck. Her breasts were small and hard as walnuts.

Cord shoved her away. He snatched up her shirt in one hand and her elbow in the other, opened the door and threw her out, tossed the shirt in her face. She clutched it to her chest.

"You ought to be ashamed of yourself, girl," Cord said, waving his fingers like the schoolmaster in a farce . . . and Chi came around the corner at the end of the hall, heading for her room.

There was Cord, in drooping long johns, gaping like a fish and his cautionary finger in midair . . . and there was Chi, folded up with laughter.

Kelsey looked at them both and fled.

Cord stomped into his room and slammed the door. He could hear Chi trying to stifle her laughter, and finally the door of her room open and close. Even so, as he got back into bed and pulled the quilt to his chin, he felt righteous and strong, and still goddamned lucky.

Chapter Nineteen

CORD AWOKE FROM DREAMLESS SLEEP CLEAR-headed and hungry, a little stiff from the long hours in the saddle the previous day but all there and himself, no hangover. Going to bed the night before a fight without being gut-full of whiskey: there was some invention.

The smell of the sulphur brought him all the way awake. The room was chill from the misty night, and Cord settled for splashing water onto his face before pulling on his shirt and britches and dry jacket. It was dawn of a dirty-looking day. Rain fell steadily from a slate-gray sky, the fat drops sizzling into the pools on the hot-spring terrace. Steam drifted everywhere.

From his window, Cord saw Abraham Buskirk heading out west across the swinging suspension bridge, a bedroll tied on behind his saddle, off to find his Arapaho pinochle partners. Buskirk turned his horse on the opposite bench and studied his sulphurous kingdom. He spotted Cord and waved, looking a little shame-faced at ducking the fight. But Cord held no resentment; he admired the old man for pulling off a feat of extraordinary survival in a changing West.

No one was in the big sitting room when Cord came down, although fresh dry wood crackled in the fireplace. He followed the smell of fresh coffee through the dining room and found Kelsey behind the high counter of the kitchen. She handed over a cup.

"You shamed me last night, Mr. Cord." Her eyes were cast down. "Made me feel small."

Her candor arrested him. Cord had thought he'd been the one to play the fool. "You forget last night."

Kelsey looked up, wet-eyed as a puppy. "I got grub on." She nodded past Cord. "Kyle and Miss Chi are waiting yonder."

They were at the table behind the wood stove, where a fire was crackling. At their elbows were placemats and flatware and spotless white linen serviettes, and between them was another pewter coffeepot. Greer was talking in a low voice and Chi was listening with something like fascination, as if hidden within his mad chatter were coded truths. This rubbed Cord against the grain, Chi paying attention to a fool. Even if they killed Ryker, they were still in trouble; Cord was busting with frustration that wanted some fit outlet....

Greer shut up when Cord sat down, and Chi carefully bit off a smart remark about his ridiculous getup the night before. "'Morning," Cord muttered.

Greer leaned toward him. "You did me a good turn that day on the North Platte," he said. "Letting me loose before you worked on Ryker." He sounded halfway lucid.

"Then why did you go back, boy?"

"Don't remember," Greer said. "But I remember that

damned night. He got me anyway, didn't he, good and proper."

"Are you going to be all right?" Cord demanded. "Can you carry any weight at all when trouble starts?"

Greer looked at Cord idiotically, and Cord saw the lucidity drift. "He tells me what to do," Greer said. "I hear his voice talking in my head."

"*Los manos de Dios*," Chi said. "Touched by God's hand. Those voices in his head, the *Indios* think it is the true word of the Lord."

"What do you think?" Cord asked sharply.

Chi deliberated. "I think he is *loco*."

"Good for you," Cord said, "because this is sure as hell no day for nonsense about God's hands." Men's hands would decide this fight, with guns.

Kelsey came through the kitchen door carrying two plates on each arm. She dealt them out and took a chair. On each platter were three fried eggs and a thick slab of bright red corned beef. Greer was captivated by the sight of his food. He cut one of his eggs down the middle, folded it over, sopped up the oozing yellow, cut a square of corned beef, impaled it on his egg-filled fork, and shoveled the dripping stack into his mouth. He chewed vigorously, absorbed by the ritual completeness of this transaction. Kelsey smiled at him, like a wife gauging the depth of her husband's love by his appetite.

Cord dusted his eggs with pepper and dug in. The corned beef was salty, but otherwise the food was hot and good. They ate in silence, and when they were done Kelsey refilled coffee cups and Chi rolled cigarettes. This room irritated Cord; the tourist appointments that had bemused him the previous night looked stupid and annoying in daylight.

"Where does that swinging bridge lead?" he asked.

Kelsey looked up brightly. "It hooks up with the main

wagon road, the one the tourist folk take down from Greybull, just over the rise. Ryker won't come from there—the Indian'll be following your track, and Ryker will follow the Indian."

"I figured that—I wasn't thinking of Ryker." Cord looked at Chi. "We could cross that bridge, though it's an idea I hate." Through cracks in plank decking, Cord saw rapids swirling fifty feet down. "But we could do it just the same, cut the ropes behind us and dump that bridge in the river."

"He'd find us," Kelsey bleated. They had to kill Ryker for her; that was the heart of her plan. "That Mr. Earl would pick up our trail."

"He is only talking, *hermana*." Chi smiled at Cord. "Aren't you?"

She was right. By the end of the next day at the latest, they would be worse off than when they had started, chased beyond this safe haven deep into wilderness, until their horses died and everyone was out of ideas, short of basic dry-gulching.

"We got food and fire and dry clothes, under a good roof. Wherever Ryker put up last night, some scared nester's soddy or whatever, he's going to be cold and wet and getting impatient. Now it is us who can do the waiting out. Let's see how he likes it," Chi said.

"Maybe. Ryker has pledged five years on this chase already. He will probably try to pull some stunt."

"Just the same," Chi sighed, "we got no choice."

"Not for long, if we are lucky." Cord wondered if he were being drawn into this impatience by a clear mind. Maybe he was better off with a numbing hangover. Maybe one drink right now, some of that Vicksburg bourbon in his coffee. Maybe that was a poor idea . . .

"He'll be in," Kyle Greer said.

Everyone looked at him.

"This ain't Fort Laramie," Greer said, sounding sane enough. "Over that ridge behind us there is maybe a half dozen deer trails, no brush to speak of, but he has got the cover of rain and steam and this ugly day ain't never going to get much lighter than it is now. He is out there, him and his faggot Pearl and the rest of them."

"Hush, boy," Chi said quietly.

"Kyle can tell," Kelsey said. "He has got what they call a sixth sense." Kelsey put her tiny hand on Cord's forearm. "Will you do it?"

Cord pulled his arm away, and Chi made an impatient noise. The question was pointless now. Enos Ryker meant to kill them, without compromise or parley. Now there was only the fight. Kelsey's fondest wish was about to come true, unless the Ryker bastard got real lucky . . .

"When Ryker is dead," Cord said, "we still got trouble to spare."

"A bank job and two murder charges." Chi nodded. "But there is nothing for it, Cord, not right this minute. We will worry about clearing our good names after we see to Ryker."

"There you are," Greer said. "Good names . . ."

Crazed mutterings were something Cord could not at the moment abide. He pointed a finger at Kelsey. "You keep a rein on him, girl." Cord lowered the finger, reminded of the silliness of the previous night. "Once this gets rolling, I want no trouble with bedlamites."

"Except Ryker," Greer said soberly.

"I am losing my patience, boy," Cord growled.

"Listen," Greer said. He touched two fingers to his forehead and closed his eyes.

"You shut up!" Cord pushed back his chair.

"*Momento*," Chi said. "Can't you hear?" Chi stood and went through the archway into the front room. Cord followed her, thinking dark thoughts about Mexican women and demented boys who shared visions. Kelsey trailed after him, but Kyle Greer kept his seat, as if there was nothing happening he could not already see.

Cord found Chi on the porch, staring up at the terraces rising beyond the bathhouse. Rain slanted down from the flat colorless sky, and clouds of steam wafted across the sulphur-covered rock shelves, alternately draping and revealing parts of the eerie otherworld that was Buskirk's little enclave.

Chi pointed into the mist. Cord peered hard and saw nothing at first, but then the wind gusted and the curtains of steam parted. For a moment Cord could see all the way along the line of the wooden aqueduct where it cut along the terrace's edges, climbing a couple hundred feet to the bowl's east ridge.

Mr. Earl stood above the steaming shelves, arms folded and still as a wax model in a nickel museum. Rain splattered off his cocked top hat and his bare chest and ran off fringes of his buckskin leggings and the folded uppers of his soft leather boots. The Indian looked down at them and nodded once.

Cord felt the irritability and impatience drain from him like rain off oilcloth. "Come on," he said. "Let's see to business."

Chapter Twenty

THE BATHHOUSE WAS A CAVERNOUS GHOSTLY shell fifty yards long and half as wide. A high corrugated tin canopy ceiling was mounted on six-by-twelve beams; a six-foot canvas modesty wall open at the top was tacked to the post. A narrow plank deck rimmed the huge dark pool, which was empty except for a few inches of rain-seep in the bottom. The pool's curved walls were fashioned of heat-warped boards sealed with pitch.

The aqueduct entered at the far end, opening into a wide chute; when the sluice gates on the terraces above were opened, hot water would fill the pool in a few hours. On either side of the intake were doors leading to dressing rooms.

Cord stood in the shadow of the doorway at the opposite end. He carried a Winchester .44 carbine borrowed from Buskirk. Guns were not a problem now: Chi had the rifle taken off the dead Payne boy, and Kelsey had her own

Winchester. In the front room of the hotel, Cord had watched her fumble cartridges into its magazine with twitching fingers.

"You going to be all right, girl?" Cord asked.

"I killed a man," she reminded him. Her plain boyish face was pale. But once the fight began, she would have to care for herself like everyone else.

"Okay," Cord had said, and was buttoning up his jacket and on the way out when Greer came to life.

"I want my shotgun," he said.

"Just what we need," Cord muttered. "Another crank with a gun."

"I got a right," Greer said reasonably. "I want Ryker bad as anyone." Greer stood. "Give me my gun, Mr. Cord."

Cord went behind the front desk and got the sawed-off shotgun. He tossed it to Greer, who caught it by the stock. "We'll maybe need the extra gun, boy," Cord said, "but if you hear any voices, make sure you listen carefully before shooting. Think first."

Now, from the shadow of the bathhouse door, Cord threw a hi-sign to Chi, positioned atop the three-story hotel. Greer and Kelsey were holed up below in the lobby, ready to move with the fight. Cord wanted them together; she could maybe keep him pointed straight ahead for the next twenty minutes or so.

Cord held the rifle against his chest and went through the bathhouse door. He cat-footed along the desk, crouching so his hat did not show above the canvas modesty wall. He passed the door and eased behind the cover of the aqueduct.

Mr. Earl remained on the ridge above the top terrace, impassive as a marble bust. Cord rose to his full height. Mr. Earl's dark head, framed by the loops of his braids, turned slowly as a lighthouse beacon. His red-tinted spectacles were opaque in the odd light and speckled with raindrops. Steam swirled around his leggings. Mr. Earl touched two fingers to his temple and nodded. The steam rose up thicker and obscured him.

Behind Cord, a boot scraped board.

Cord whirled and stepped back and went down on one knee. A rifle cracked and a slug punched through the dressing room door. One of the Payne boys, on the deck across the corner of the pool, was working the lever of his rifle.

Cord fired the carbine one handed from the hip, rushing the shot, but the Payne boy flopped forward anyway and slid face first down the curve of the empty pool's wall. Cord rose cautiously and went around toward where he had fallen.

A rifle fired from the direction of the hotel, and the other Payne boy came through the door at a dead run. Cord fired at him as the other man slipped on the sulphur-slime coating the decking, dropping his rifle over the lip of the pool. The man was up and running instantly. Cord worked the rifle's lever, tracked onto him, got the spot between his shoulder blades in the open sights, and swore and did not fire.

The gunman threw his shoulder into the door of the woman's dressing room and crashed on through. The door rebounded and slammed shut behind him.

Cord was already moving around the corner of the pool. He put three slugs through the door, fast as he could fire, then planted his boot in the middle of the door and went in low.

He saw a row of wash basins along one side wall, a line of shower stalls along the other, and four dressing cubicles in front of him, each with a closed canvas curtain hanging from a rod. Cord fired waist-high into the curtain on the left, levered, fired into the next one, levered again.

The curtain on the far right exploded outward and the Payne boy came through, waving a revolver. Cord shot him in the chest, and the Payne boy half turned and clawed at the canvas curtain. Its rod broke in the middle and the heavy canvas fell over him like a shroud.

A shot sounded from the hotel. Cord went out, rifle ready, round the corner of the pool.

It was empty. No Payne boys were lying facedown in the bilge water. The damned carbine . . . Cord was used to a longer gun and must have merely creased the other gunman.

Across the yard, Kelsey screamed.

Nothing moved in the open space between the bathhouse and the hotel's porch. The fire in the hearth threw flickering shadows across the windows. Cord drew two quick breaths and dog-trotted for it, rifle up and ready. No one shot at him until he was halfway there.

The bullet splashed into a puddle a foot in front of him. Cord zigzagged and belly-flopped behind a horse trough. Mud splattered his face.

"Cord!" Ryker screamed "You are under arrest, you murdering son of a bitch. Throw out that carbine and show yourself."

Cord kept still. There were wisps of steam everywhere, but the rainwater pool in which he lay was frigid.

"I got the girl and Greer," Ryker called, "and your partner is treed. So you come in here and take your medicine, bucko."

Cord took off his hat and peered above the lip of the trough. The door was open, but he could see no one.

"First thing is . . . I'll shoot the girl and then the fruitcake," Ryker called from inside. "Then I will torch this place and cook your partner like a suckling pig. You ever hear of a hot piece of ass, Mr. Cord?" Ryker guffawed.

Chi appeared at the edge of the roof. She was okay, and not half treed; one end of sixty feet of strong hemp rope was tied around the chimney. She glared at Cord and shook her head no. Cord nodded assent: soon as he gave himself up to Ryker, they were in the fat.

A bullet cored through the water trough. Cord ducked down, pressed his face into the dirty water.

Ryker was in the doorway now, backlit by the fire's flow, ducked down behind Kelsey. He held her arm cranked up toward her shoulders, and the muzzles of the shotgun jammed into the underside of her chest. Her child's face was screwed up with the pain of it.

"I'm edgy, Cord." Ryker was grinning madly. "My nerves are all a-jumping." He jerked Kelsey's arm and she yelped.

Cord thought sickly, *he will do it*.

"Say your prayers, bitch," Ryker growled.

Cord threw the carbine over the trough, stood and moved toward the porch.

Ryker laughed again. He whipped Kelsey around and flung her through the door behind him. She sprawled on the floor. Ryker kept the shotgun on Cord.

From the corner of his eye Cord saw Chi move back from the edge of the roof.

Ryker gestured with the gun. "Come ahead, boy." Cord stepped up on the porch and Ryker moved to one side, ramming the shotgun painfully into Cord's kidneys to shove him inside.

Kelsey was on hands and knees, her head hanging groggily. Kyle Greer perched, immobile, on the edge of one of the armchairs, was squeezing his hands between his knees and staring at the floor. The last Payne cousin covered him. There was blood on his jacket where Cord's slug had creased his ribs, but he was not hurt badly enough to matter.

Bernard Pearl was behind the bar, where he could watch the whole room. He wore the same clothes as he had in Denver a week earlier, and he stank all over. His greasy hair was clotted with trail dust, like bugs on lantern glass. Cord stared at him until his Adam's apple bobbed in his chicken neck and he looked away.

Kelsey picked herself up, angrily ignoring Cord's proffered hand. The pressure in his kidneys went away, along with the weight of his holstered Peacemaker. Ryker stuck the revolver in the front of his belt and gestured Cord over toward the fireplace next to Greer, who was muttering inaudibly.

"Got you good, Cord," Ryker said thickly.

"Get it done with," Pearl spat. "We want away from this goddamned stink. Place smells real nasty."

"You'd know," Cord said.

"Kill him," Pearl said flatly.

Ryker spun around and fixed the shotgun on Pearl. "Kill you, you freak. Kill you right now if you don't shut your mouth."

Pearl threw up both hands.

"Do this right," Ryker muttered to himself. He turned back to Cord. "Call your woman down."

"You call her down," Cord said. "See what happens."

"Tell what will happen." Ryker moved to the foot of the stairs, raised his voice. "I'll shoot your leg off." He craned his neck and called up the stairwell in a giddy thrill-crazed voice. "You hear that, bitch? I'll put one load in his knees and the other in his balls, unless you are down here double-quick."

Ryker ran his forefinger along the ridge of the scar on his cheek, where Chi had cut him five years before. "Gonna do her first, this time for sure. You're gonna watch, smell her sweat and lather." Ryker's voice was singsong, as if he were reciting. "Then I will shoot you a piece at a time, her turn to watch. Do her again before I kill her." Spittle flecked from Ryker's thick lips. Even Payne looked at him strangely.

"Last chance, bitch!" Ryker screamed up the stairs.

Kyle Greer moaned like a tormented soul and toppled face forward off the edge of the armchair, stiff as a stick. He hit the floor and rolled on his back, his eyes up in his head, and began twitching all over as if possessed.

Cord dropped to one knee beside him. Ryker stared with irritation at the interruption. Greer was gasping like a fish on a hot rock. Cord held his mouth open and tried to feel if he had swallowed his tongue.

But Greer could breath after all, because the gasping stopped for a moment and Cord heard, "Front desk." Cord drew up and stared, but Greer was gulping for air again, and jerking his arms and legs like a holy roller.

"Help me with him," Cord said, thinking, *Greer's shotgun, nowhere in sight . . .*

"I'll help him," Ryker said, and shot Greer. Greer moaned and flopped over on his stomach, leaking blood and not moving.

Another gunshot sounded quick as an echo and a window shattered. Ryker and his man Payne turned and ducked.

Cord had been waiting for Chi's move. He launched himself over the top of the front desk. One shoulder crashed painfully into the letter rack as he went down, but there on the shelf was Greer's God-blessed shotgun.

A rifle fired inside the room and an answering shot broke more window glass. Someone cried out. By that time Cord was coming up, both barrels of the shotgun cocked.

The last Payne cousin fell over backward and his right arm flopped into the fire. Bernard Pearl squealed and ducked behind the bar. Cord unloosed one barrel in his general direction, and Pearl screamed and began to sob.

Ryker was gone. Cord went through the archway to the dining room. It was empty, but the back door of the kitchen rattled loose in the wind.

Chi was coming in the door as he returned to the lobby. Kelsey came out from behind the cover of a sofa. Greer lay still as death, and Pearl went on weeping like a child, out of sight behind the oak bar front. The Payne boy lay open-eyed with the blood all over his chest. His smoking coat sleeve burst into flame, and the char of burning flesh rose above the sulphur fumes. Chi dragged the body clear and put out the flaming jacket with a throw rug.

Kelsey cried out and knelt by Kyle Greer. Pearl sobbed, "Help me, for the love of God."

The hell with him. Cord went back into the dining room and through the kitchen to the open door.

"Goddamn it, Cord, you wait." Chi stood arms akimbo on the other side of the high counter.

Cord knew: she hated Ryker for many things, but most of all for making her the object of his filthy fantasies. She wanted him for herself.

"You see to Greer and Pearl," Cord ordered in a hard voice. He was cutting her out of this now; she was too wound up, enough anyway to let anger cloud good sense. "Just shut your mouth and do what I say."

She glared back for three seconds, then turned and went back into the lobby. Cord could not have been more surprised if she had stripped naked. There remained only one piece of unfinished business.

Cord went out the kitchen door into the rain, in time to spot Ryker, across the yard and turning behind the livery barn, raising a flurry of chickens. *Bastard is carrying my gun*, Cord thought, and thought about turning back for more firepower.

There was no time. Unless Ryker was turning dumb, he had horses picketed on the other side of the ridge.

Cord meant to have him; letting Ryker escape was out of the question. This fight was going to be finished; they would divide the murder charges afterward over coffee. Ryker, the conniving son of a bitch.

"Ryker!" Cord shouted into the rain.

At the corner of the barn the sawed-off shotgun's muzzle flared. Pellets from the wasted shell rained on the yard between them. Ryker fled behind the barn toward the bathhouse.

Cord cut in front of the barn and saw Ryker duck inside the bathhouse. He heard the heavy tattoo of Ryker's boots on the decking and followed the sound, running outside along the canvas wall.

Cord ducked up the stairs beside the woman's dressing room, his finger taut against the shotgun's back trigger. Ryker was gone. Cord stood still and strained his ears. From the rush of the springs cascading over the terraces and the hiss of rain turning to steam, he sorted out another sound: something scraping wood.

Ryker was halfway up the three-foot-wide trough of the empty aqueduct, climbing to the ridge less than a hundred feet above. He turned and tossed a pistol shot at Cord, hitting five feet wide, then scurried on, scuttling on all fours like a crab.

There were six terraces, giant stairsteps a yard high and five yards deep, covered in a thick coating of egg-yellow slime; the wooden aqueduct ran diagonally up one side at perhaps a twenty-degree angle. Each terrace was covered with a broad sheet of flowing water, and at each crossing a sluice gate was set into the uphill side. Cord tucked the shotgun under his arm and started up after Ryker.

Ryker shot a look over his shoulder. He scrambled up another couple of steps and opened the sluice gate at the third terrace. A few inches of steaming water came pouring down and washed over Cord's boots. He got a grip on one edge of the flume, pulled himself up, and went after Ryker.

Ryker opened the sluice gate at the fourth terrace and moved on. The water rose above Cord's ankles, and the wood planking grew slick as if greased. He held on against the flow and peered upward, but a billow of steam obscured Ryker. Cord plowed up into it.

Ryker's shotgun boomed and pellets tore the steam. One stung Cord's cheek, another tore across the back of his right hand. He let go of the sawed-off shotgun and it splashed into the roiling hot water. Cord lunged after it, got two fingers around the muzzle, and reeled it back in, wondering if the remaining charge was any good.

A pistol shot missed Cord by a foot. He looked up in time to see Ryker's empty shotgun skimming down the aqueduct dead at him. Cord swung himself aside and the long gun flew past like a lance. By then Ryker had opened the gate at the fifth terrace. The water rose to Cord's knees, plucking at his footing like an evil spirit. Ryker was no more than fifty feet above him. Cord pushed against the flow.

Ryker clawed his way to the top of the aqueduct and opened the headgate.

A wall of 135-degree water a yard wide and a foot high came frothing at Cord, and he dropped the shotgun and grabbed the lip of the chute with both hands. The water hit a moment later.

It was scalding hot; Cord felt his skin tighten, and felt the quick blistering pain. He got a leg over the edge of the flume, pulled himself mostly clear of the flow, and immediately began to shiver in the rain.

Ryker climbed over the headgate and got his footing. He turned and brought up Cord's Peacemaker. Cord saw Ryker's ugly grin above the sights, as he carefully lined the barrel on Cord where he clung twenty feet below.

A rifle cracked and a thin liquid line of red spurted from

the center of Ryker's chest. Ryker dropped Cord's Peacemaker into the flume and it swept down the chute. He took a half step backward, overcompensated, and his knees caught the headgate.

Ryker tumbled forward stiff as a tree, face first into the flood of water pouring into the chute. He swept down head first like a log in a flume and rocketed past Cord, careening downchute. Cord turned in time to see Ryker fly over the lip of the pool and heard his corpse thump hollowly on the wooden bottom.

Cord stared up through the steam and rain, and there behind the headgate stood Chi, her Winchester dribbling black smoke.

Cord shook his head wearily as Chi shut down the water. He wiped at his cheek with the back of his hand and saw blood smeared there. His fingers made out the shape of a little lump of lead below the first layer of skin, and when he pinched, it popped out. Cord flung it away. By then the water flow had become manageable, and Cord dropped back into the trough and began to make his way carefully down, hand over hand.

Chapter Twenty-One

THE LOBBY LOOKED LIKE A HOSPITAL WARD, but no one was going to die. Kyle Greer was hurt worst: the heavy .45 slug had shattered his collarbone before passing out through his shoulder, and he had to be in considerable pain though he did not reveal it. His face was pale, but he was sitting up and breathing only a bit raggedly. Kelsey had bandaged the entrance and exit wounds and was rigging a sling from two kitchen towels.

"It was my fault," Kelsey said to no one in particular, though Greer turned his head and looked up at her blankly. "I was keeping my eye on Kyle, right up to when Ryker stabbed that double-barrel into my butt." She looked at Cord, leaning on the bar. "Kyle was acting up, so I took his shotgun and put it back behind the desk."

"That was a break," Cord said.

"I'm okay," Greer said suddenly, his voice scratchy and mechanical.

Cord stared through him. "Ryker spotted me when I crossed to the bathhouse," he reasoned aloud. "He sent the Payne cousins to keep me busy, while him and our Mr. Pearl here snuck up on the girl and Greer."

Pearl moaned at the mention of his name. He sat slumped in an armchair.

"Shut up, Mr. Pearl," Cord said amiably. "That fine bar is hurt worse than you." One end of the fancy bar was splintered and bashed in, where most of Cord's wild shotgun blast had lit. Cord remembered Buskirk's admonition and shook his head ruefully.

"Lordy, I am dying," Pearl groaned. "You are talking money, and I am dying." The edge of Cord's close-range shotgun pattern had stitched a six-inch crescent of buckshot into Pearl's thigh. One of his stovepipe pant legs was torn off at the thigh, and from there to the knee the meaty part of Pearl's left haunch looked like it had been chewed on by a large carnivore.

"You are not going to die, Mr. Pearl," Cord said. "Not so long as you get to a doctor and have him dig the lead out before it starts to fester. My partner can't work on you— her knife is likely to slip. Jesus!"

His right hand was palm-down on the bartop, and Chi was digging a small hole in its back with the tip of her knife. Cord swigged from the bottle of Old Vicksburg at his elbow. The fight was won, and he had the excuse of pain.

"Oh, Lordy," Pearl whined.

"Goddamn it, Pearl, shut up," Cord snapped. "Have a goddamned drink." Maybe he was already moving toward drunk. Maybe, hell.

Cord pulled his hand away from Chi. He grabbed the bottle by the neck and took it to where Pearl sat slumped. Pearl's celluloid collar was lost somewhere along the trail, and his cardboard shirt front was rain-soaked and curled up under his chin. Pearl licked his lips and reached for the bottle.

Cord jerked it back and clamped a hand around Pearl's mutilated thigh. He kneaded the flesh and Pearl screamed. Cord let go and grabbed a fistful of Pearl's jacket, jerking him up straight. Pearl bleated and Cord splashed whiskey over the open wound. Pearl screamed again, like a woman.

"Don't you worry, Mr. Pearl," Cord said. "We are going to have you in the hospital in Greybull before dark. We are your guardian angels. We are going to trust you with a lot of money, maybe our lives."

Kelsey shot a look at Cord.

"You are going to turn the bank money over to the law," Cord went on in Pearl's face. "Then you are going to tell them the story, the whole goddamned truth. You will leave out the girl and Greer here—you don't know who playacted as us, because Ryker didn't tell you—but you damned sure tell all the rest."

"If I do, I am done."

"If you don't, I will kill you." Cord drew his Colt, fished out of the pool and now clean and fresh-loaded. He laid the muzzle against Pearl's forehead. "Kill you right now," Cord hissed. He thumbed back the hammer.

Bernard Pearl looked into Cord's hard eyes and fainted. Cord threw him back into the chair. Some of Pearl's blood stained Cord's hand. He wiped it off across the front of Pearl's tight jacket and laughed.

"You done?" Chi inquired. She was waiting at the bar, her knife poised. Cord, a little sheepishly, put his hand back in front of her. She dug into him and then the pellet was glistening red on the point of her knife. The sum of the damage was a quarter-inch crater in the back of Cord's hand.

He splashed bourbon over it and yelped at the sting. It was Chi's turn to laugh.

She nodded at Pearl. "Will he do it?"

"He'd better," Cord said grimly.

"*Sí*," Chi said, "but it still might not clear us."

Cord shrugged. "We'll see." It was as good a plan as he could come up with right now. Even with Pearl backing them, they could not risk surrendering to the law, not just yet. They were riding ahead of too much bad history, and Cord had no time to waste in someone's jail. Maybe after the foofaraw calmed they could find a trustworthy lawman and tell him their side of the tale with half a chance of making it stick.

Chi turned toward the door and said, "Company is coming."

Cord heard nothing, but then someone hollered, "Hallo, the lodge!"

"The *viejo*." Chi went to the door. "Come ahead," she called.

Buskirk stopped in the doorway and took a look around. He lingered on Kyle Greer's bandages, Cord's bleeding hand, Pearl's torn-up leg. "Who is dead?" he asked cheerfully.

Cord was easing down from the blood-percolating charge of the fight and wearying of that sort of humor. "Ryker and two Payne cousins. Pearl here is going to live to tell the truth."

"He is your alibi?"

"Yeah," Cord said glumly. "He isn't much, is he."

Buskirk bent over his fine Long Bar and ran his fingers over the splintered end panel.

"Charge it to our bill," Cord said.

"I will," Buskirk replied mildly. "But maybe I will leave

the damage as it is, for the tourists to goggle at. I'll make up a story."

"Don't put me in it," Chi warned.

"Well now." Buskirk dry-washed his hands. "What happens?"

"Some burying," Cord said. "Then we dump Pearl in Greybull and ride north." Cord nodded at Greer and Kelsey. "Don't know about them."

"They'll stay on here for a time," Buskirk said. "Take a little resort vacation like real folk—do 'em good."

Kelsey nodded. Greer was gone somewhere in his head, had been since the moment he'd tipped Cord to the shotgun and been shot for his trouble.

"Me and Kyle will do the burying," Buskirk said. "Give the boy something to occupy his mind."

Kelsey let go of Greer. "You want the money," she said.

Cord looked away and scowled. Chi said gently, "We need it more than you, *hija*."

"Do you? Never mind; I'll fetch it." But for a moment she did not move, except to contemplate Kyle Greer. "I can make him well," she said. When no one answered, she turned up the stairs.

In the livery barn, Cord let the mechanical tasks of saddling blank his mind for a few minutes. Chi was on the porch when he brought the horses around. Pearl stood woozily next to her, hands tied. Cord hoisted him into the saddle and looped a tether rope around the bonds wrapping his wrists, then mounted the bay and led them toward the swinging suspension bridge.

"Adios," Buskirk called. Kelsey stood beside him on the porch. "Come back sometime—you get special rates if you stay the week."

Cord hated the swaying bridge, but managed by staring rigidly ahead and trusting the bay not to pitch him into the void. He led Pearl up on the opposite bench and let out his breath.

But then Chi turned and trotted back across the narrow span, easy as if she were riding down a prairie wagon-track. She was fine on an animal, Cord thought. She reined up on the other side. *"Hermana!"*

Kelsey came running. Cord watched Chi bend in the saddle and put her head close to Kelsey's. Chi reached under her serape. Kelsey smiled and kissed Chi awkwardly on the lips. Chi swung her mare around and crossed the bridge once more.

They rode north in silence for several miles, Pearl oozing in and out of consciousness. Given the last few days Cord felt good enough, on the whole. At least they were on the road and heading with the spring to Montana, he and Chi. Another piece of gunman's luck.

Cord thumped the gelding and pulled up beside Chi. *"Cuanto, amiga?"*

"Two thousand," Chi said. "You think it was too much?"

"About right." Cord looked off left toward the mountains. "Anyway, there are things more important than money."

Chi laughed. "Let us go to Montana, *querido*." She rode ahead to lead the way.

Afterword

JOE LEFORS MET TOM HORN IN THE FALL OF 1901 in Frank Meanea's saddle shop in Cheyenne. The two men were a study in contrasts. LeFors was several inches under six feet, and wore a bow tie, a waxed walrus mustache, and a three-piece suit with the signet of a fraternal organization on his watch fob. He had clean, vaguely Germanic features, and at the age of thirty-six was growing a bit soft above the belt. He looked like a cop.

Tom Horn was six feet two inches tall and weighed 206 pounds, with broad sinewy shoulders and a slab-flat stomach. Five years older than LeFors, he wore trail clothing and worn boots. His thin hair was beginning to recede, and below his high forehead were small hard eyes that seemed long divorced from anything like humor. He looked like bad news.

Horn was picking up a scabbard that Meanea had custom-crafted for his .30-30, and to make conversation the two men discussed the finer points—sighting accuracy, muzzle velocity, penetration power—of the popular Winchester lever-action rifle. LeFors found his new acquaintance "well posted on small arms and rather inclined to brag." After a time the two men shook hands and went their separate ways.

LeFors and Horn, strangers until this meeting, had lived similar lives, but now they worked different sides of the road. Joe LeFors was a U.S. Deputy Marshal, and Tom Horn, with his dark mean eyes, was the last and most deadly hired gun in the West.

The tenacity of the character of Enos Ryker in *Gunsmoke River* is inspired by Joe LeFors, although it should be noted that there is no hint of Ryker-like corruption in the true-life marshal. LeFors was born in 1865 to farming folk in Paris, in the northeast corner of Texas. He was the fourth of five brothers. His father James J., a Kentuckian, was fifty-seven that year, and his mother, Mahala Wester, a native of Tennessee, was thirty-eight. In 1878, the family moved to the Texas Panhandle, where it farmed outside Mobeetie on the Sweetwater River, in the area of the present-day town of LeFors, and by 1880, both parents were dead.

During the next five years LeFors was a freighter, mail-route rider, and cowboy. He learned to handle a ten-yoke oxen team, work cattle, and adroitly avoid the renegade bands of hostile natives who frequently left the reservations in the Indian Territories to rustle range cattle and, when the spirit moved them, attack isolated white ranchers and riders.

In the spring of 1885, LeFors signed on with the H Bar Y Ranch at Gageby Creek east of Mobeetie. Hitting the trail on April 10, the H Bar Y crew drove 2,900 head of yearlings and two-year-olds 1,000 miles north across open range and runoff-swollen rivers to Buffalo, Wyoming, in sixty days. LeFors, sniffing opportunity, drew his pay and took a job on a local ranch. A competent, honest, and responsible hand, he was soon promoted to foreman.

In 1890 LeFors moved north to Miles City, the eastern Montana livestock center, where he worked for the Murphy Company, which had contracted to supply over 3,000 beeves annually to the Sioux Indians at the Standing Rock Agency. LeFors learned both Sioux and the hand-signing language that served as a *lingua franca* among different tribes and whites, and says that the Sioux named him "Tiatonka Che," or Beef Chief.

Miles City was the headquarters of W. D. Smith, chief investigator for the Montana Live Stock Association. On Smith's recommendation, LeFors was offered a job as brand inspector, assigned to northeastern Wyoming. LeFors was looking for a new challenge and accepted. Although it would be another six years before they met face to face, another new inspector had recently taken the same position with the Wyoming Cattlemen's Association. For a time, at least, Joe LeFors and Tom Horn were colleagues.

Tom Horn was born near Memphis, Scotland County, Missouri, on November 21, 1860, and ran away from home at the age of fourteen, after his father had beaten him so badly he spent a week in bed. A job as a teamster took Horn to New Mexico, where he quit to drive an Overland Mail stagecoach between Santa Fe and Prescott, Arizona. At the time, the Western and Chiricahua Apaches were waging perhaps the most viciously effective guerrilla war any native tribe ever launched against Europeans, and Horn's job should have been somewhere between perilous and suicidal. He managed to survive through luck and go-to-hell brass, and by age sixteen was fluent in Apache and Spanish. That skill, and the recommendation of Al Sieber, the famous German-born Indian-fighter, got Horn a job with the U.S. Army.

For the next ten years, Horn and Sieber worked out of Fort Whipple as scouts, translators, and mercenaries.

Geronimo's surrender ended the Apache Wars and idled Horn. Still well under thirty, he served as a deputy sheriff for a time, and rodeoed on the side, taking the steer-roping buckle at Phoenix one year. In 1890 Horn joined the Pinkerton Detective Agency. He was credited with breaking up the McCoy gang, a notorious bunch of murdering train robbers, but Horn later claimed that he never liked Pinkerton work. His trail finally led him to Wyoming and a job which was not so different from what he was used to. By 1894, Tom Horn had lived by his gun for twenty of his thirty-four years.

The profession to which Joe LeFors and Tom Horn turned within a year of each other was variously called "brand inspector," "range detective," or "livestock investigator." The employer was either a stockgrowers' organization or a single large rancher, and the inspector had no official law enforcement status. His general instruction was to protect the financial interests of his boss, but methodology and the lengths to which an inspector carried his mandate varied from man to man.

One stockgrower concern was nesters, small ranchers who took advantage of the several Homestead Acts to claim, settle, and often fence off prime sections of bottomland range with access to year-round water. Although claiming no legal title to the land, the big ranchers did claim the rights of usage, eminent domain, and capitalist prerogative.

In some areas, sheep were another worry. Grazing woolies crop grass close to the ground's surface, and cowmen believed that this irredeemably ruined the range. The fact that they were wrong did not stop them from harassing sheepherders and their flocks.

Finally, there was rustling, an unfortunate term that once innocuously meant "gathering," as in "rustling up some grub." There were surely those who stole cattle and horses as an ongoing criminal enterprise; indeed, Joe LeFors was assigned by his Montana bosses to the Powder River country of Wyoming because it was a major corridor for driving stolen Montana stock to the famous robbers' roost at Hole-in-the-Wall. But some stockmen used the accusation of rustling as a general weapon in what was essentially an economic war. The basically honest rancher who ignored the brand on a cow or two during spring roundup was technically a thief, though hardly a threat to order. Among the utterly blameless were those who ranched near rustler hole-ups and kept their traps shut out of neighborliness and prudence, and those who were simply getting in a local stockgrower's hair. For a more complete discussion of the complexities of the rustler question, see our Afterword to *Hunt the Man Down*, the fifth book in the "Cord" series.

Despite the similarity of title, Joe LeFors and Tom Horn had different mandates. LeFors's assignment was to recover stolen Montana cattle which had been driven across the border into Wyoming, and to obtain convictions of the cow thieves as a deterrent to others with the same idea. Tom Horn combatted professional rustlers too, but a significant part of his job was to intimidate and sometimes drive out nesters and sheepmen.

Further, Lefors and Horn brought different points of view to their work. LeFors believed in an honest day's work and the sanctity of property rights. He was a meticulous detective with an eye for detail, and his successful cases are marked by doggedness rather than brilliant deductive leaps of imagination. He concentrated on the professional bunches, and was with the small army that finally breached Hole-in-the-Wall in 1897. Although locals were invited to come forward to make ownership claims, none did, for the excellent reason that the cattle rounded up were patently stolen. Five hundred head bore the brands of Wyoming and Montana cattle companies; fifty head had had brands clumsily altered, and on another twenty-eight steers the brands had been knife-skinned from the living animal and the edges sewn together. Later, LeFors was a member of the posse that trailed Butch Cassidy's Wild Bunch after it blew up the express car on the Overland Flyer. Around 1900, LeFors accepted a commission as a Deputy U.S. Marshal. His superior, Frank A. Hadsell, was a Federal appointee who spent most of his time on his sheep ranch near Rawlins, so the day-to-day marshaling fell to LeFors. In his first year, he successfully apprehended a train robber and counterfeiter.

Tom Horn, on the other hand, believed that life was a mean game with few rules, in which the deadliest son of a bitch with the most guns won. Horn saw himself as that son of a bitch. The Army had paid him to hunt down Apaches, and the Pinkertons had paid him to hunt down anyone for whom money was offered. In either case, the employer rarely cared whether the prey came in breathing or stiff. If capitalist ranchers were willing to pay to fight rustlers or rivals—or to stop them dead—Horn saw it as about the same job. "I'm an exterminatin' son of a bitch," he once proclaimed.

Hired guns were nothing new to the West when Horn sold his to the stockgrowers of Wyoming in 1894. They dated from the years immediately after the Civil War, when a lot of men with killing experience were out of work. Before the nester troubles began in the West in the mid 1880's, gunslingers worked for mining magnates with labor trouble and railroads bothered by road agents. Historian Paul Trachtman writes, "Of all the gunfighters, these mercenaries were the hardest to classify. As a group, they were neither outlaws nor lawmen, though many had pursued both careers in the past. In their role as vigilantes, they usually operated not so much in defiance of the law as simply beyond its reach."

After abortive service in the cause of the Spanish-American War (Horn caught malaria and was mustered out in Florida), Horn killed two alleged rustlers, Nigger Dart Isham and Matt Rash, in another notorious outlaw hideout, Brown's Park, near the Wyoming-Colorado-Utah border. Then, in the spring of 1901, Horn went to work for John Coble, scion of a wealthy Pennsylvania family who had given up an appointment to the U.S. Naval Academy to horse ranch at Iron Mountain, Wyoming. Coble was attracted to the romantic figure of Horn as an embodiment of the just finished century and the Old West, and put him to work searching out rustlers and other troublemakers in the neighborhood. It was Horn's perhaps overzealous execution of this assignment that led to that first meeting with Marshal Joe LeFors.

Glendolene Myrtle Kimmell was a minor though catalytic character in the drama to come. A strange little woman with almond-eyed, vaguely Oriental features who had left her Missouri home to teach at the Iron Mountain School, she idolized Horn and was his occasional lover. To a reporter for *The Cincinnati Enquirer*, she swore that Tom Horn was "a man who embodied the characteristics, the experiences, and the code of the old frontiersman."

Glendolene Kimmell boarded with the homesteading family of Victor Miller, neighbors to the family of Kels P. Nickell. Nickell had outraged nesters and big cattlemen alike by bringing in sheep; in the spring of 1901, Nickell and Miller were also feuding over a fist-fight between two of their sons at a dance. On the morning of July 18, 1901, fourteen-year-old Willie Nickell was found at the corral gate, shot dead. He was a big lad, and was wearing a low-brimmed hat and an overcoat against the early-morning high-country chill, and the murderer may have mistaken him for his father.

Tom Horn, whose reputation as a killer was so potent by now that he usually needed only to be seen riding the range to stop rustling in an area, was accused of the murder, as was Victor Miller. Horn claimed that he was on a train between Cheyenne and Laramie the day of the killing. Miller was, ironically, alibied by schoolteacher Kimmell, who testified to a coroner's jury that Miller was at his home when the killing occurred.

Seventeen days after Willie Nickell was killed, his father Kels was shot in the arm, hip, and side from ambush, and while he was in the hospital several masked men fired into his sheep herd, killing a couple dozen of the woolies. Kels Nickell finally saw the bloody handwriting on the wall, and removed to Cheyenne to work as a night watchman for the Union Pacific.

Enter Joe LeFors.

Partially through pressure from the cattlemen of the Cheyenne Club, the investigation into the Nickell shooting was eventually dropped by local lawmen, but as U.S. Marshal, LeFors considered it his duty to pursue the killer. After a time he became convinced it was Tom Horn. He knew that Horn had killed men for money; anyone who had heard Horn's barroom crowing knew that. There was a wealth of circumstantial evidence as well, although it is notable that LeFors was unable ever to prove Horn's guilt through evidence or witnesses. LeFors later admitted to Horn, "In the Willie Nickell killing I could never find your trail, and I pride myself on being a trailer."

Still, LeFors had no motive for hounding Tom Horn,

besides a belief in his guilt and a sense of justice. If LeFors were under any external pressure, it would have come from stockman's allies from the governor (who had once almost hired Horn himself) on down, and it would have pressed him to drop the case.

LeFors's investigation began while Kels Nickell was still in the hospital, when he interviewed Mrs. Mary Mahoney Nickell at the family's Iron Mountain ranch. After eliminating as suspects a half-breed barn painter and family enemy Miller, LeFors settled on Horn. It was at this point that LeFors asked Police Chief Sandy McKneal for an introduction when they spotted Horn in Meanea's saddlery.

Not long afterward, an informant told LeFors that Horn had arrived in Laramie the day of the killing on a "steamy shaken horse," and had left a blood-stained sweater at a cobbler's shop. Still, all LeFors's "evidence" remained anecdotal, hearsay, or circumstantial. Even by the investigative standards of the time, LeFors could not convict on the basis of what he had, and he knew it.

Meanwhile, Tom Horn was in Denver, drinking heavily, and avoiding Wyoming for a time. Denver was a cosmopolitan city by the turn of the century, and Horn a charming anachronism who blew loud about himself, especially when drunk. Although the faithful Glendolene Kimmell wrote to warn him that LeFors would not let the Nickell matter lie, Horn went on accepting free drinks from amused bankers and petty politicians in the Denver public houses.

At the very least, Tom Horn was a bad drunk. At worst, he may have been losing touch with reality and his own mortality. He apparently made dangerous but less than damning allusions to his role in the Nickell killing before several witnesses, despite Glendolene's warning. On another occasion, Horn abused for sport a compact citified dude who had the nerve to take the spot at the barrail next to Horn. The dude turned out to be a nationally ranked prizefighter known as "Young" Corbett. Corbett broke Horn's jaw and battered him into unconsciousness.

While Horn was drinking his meals through a straw in Denver, a woman Pinkerton working undercover with LeFors got Glendolene Kimmell liquored up. Glendolene shared Horn's fancy for hootch, braggadocio, and the confusion of reality and might-have-been, because she told the woman agent that she had brought Tom Horn sandwiches while he lay in ambush for Kels Nickell, Willie's father.

On sobering up the next morning, Glendolene must have had an inkling that she had mouthed off too much, because she sent word that she wished to see LeFors in her hotel room. There she asked point-blank if Horn was a suspect. LeFors evaded the question, assuring her only that everything would turn out all right. According to LeFors, the interview ended this way:

> I said, "Well forget our talk."
> She laughed and said, "When I sent for you, I fully intended to kill you, but I believe you are all right now." While she was talking she shook a keen-edged dagger out of her sleeve.
> "I didn't know what you wanted," I told her, "or who I was going to meet with when I was coming upstairs," and I shook an automatic (pistol) out of my sleeve. She laughed and we shook hands and declared we would be friends.
> The woman was just about as dangerous as Horn himself. I think she was about one-half Spanish or something, not entirely all-American.

Then, about the first of the year, 1902, six months after Willie Nickell died, LeFors got a letter from W. D. Smith of Miles City, his old Chief Inspector from his range detective days. Smith was looking for a "good man to do some secret work," involving rustling on the Big Moon River. The letter gave LeFors the beginnings of an idea. He forwarded it to John Coble's Iron Mountain Ranch, where Horn had returned, offering him the job.

Horn was enthusiastic. Addressing LeFors as "Friend Joe," Horn wrote back that he "would like to take up that work." He continued: "I don't care how big or bad his [W. D. Smith's] men are or how many of them there are, I can handle them . . . Put me in communication with Mr. Smith whom I know well by reputation and I can guarantee him the recommendation of every cow man in the state of Wyoming in this line of work . . . I can handle his work . . . with less expense in the shape of lawyer and witness fees than any man in the business." Horn added, "Joe you yourself know what my reputation is although we have never been out together."

It was the response—and the opportunity—LeFors had been hoping for. On Sunday, January 12, he met Horn at the Cheyenne railroad station, and from there the two cordial acquaintances went to LeFors's office for a final interview by LeFors on behalf of W. D. Smith. Parts of their conversation went this way:

HORN—"I don't want to be making reports to anybody at any time. If a man has to make reports all the time, they will catch the wisest S.O.B. on earth. These people are not afraid of shooting, are they?"
LEFORS—"No, they are not afraid of shooting."
HORN—"I shoot too much I know. You know me when it comes to shooting."

HORN—"The only thing I was ever afraid of was that I would be compelled to kill an officer, or a man I didn't want to; but I would do everything to keep from being seen, but if he kept after me, I would certainly kill him."

Horn told LeFors that he had laid in wait for Willie Nickell for at least three days, with nothing to eat except a little raw bacon. "I get so hungry that I could kill my mother for some grub," Horn said, "but I never quit a job until I get my man."

LEFORS—"How far was Willie Nickell killed?"
HORN—"About three hundred yards. It was the best shot that I ever made, and the dirtiest trick I ever done."

The two men went downstairs for a drink. They returned in fifteen minutes to finish the interview.

HORN—"The first man I killed was when I was only twenty-six years old [presumably Horn was not counting Indians]. He was a coarse S.O.B."
LEFORS—"How much did you get for killing these fellows? In the Powell and Lewis case you got six hundred dollars apiece. You killed Lewis in the corral with a six-shooter. I would like to have seen the expression on his face when you shot him." (William Lewis and Fred Powell were Iron Mountain ranchers whose 1895 slayings remained officially unsolved.)
HORN—"He was the scaredest S.O.B. you ever saw. How did you come to know that, Joe?"
LEFORS—"I have known everything you have done, Tom, for a great many years. I know where you were

paid this money on the train between Cheyenne and Denver. Why did you put the rock under the kid's head after you killed him? This is one of your marks, isn't it?"

HORN—"Yes, that is the way I hang out my sign to collect money for a job of this kind."

LEFORS—"Have you got your money yet for the killing of Nickell?"

HORN—"I got that before I did the job."

LEFORS—"You got five hundred dollars for that. Why did you cut the price?"

HORN—"I got twenty-one hundred dollars."

LEFORS—"How much is that a man?"

HORN—"That is for three dead men, and one man shot at five times. Killing is my specialty. I look at it as a business proposition, and I think I have a corner on the market."

A connecting door behind LeFors's desk led to a storeroom, and in preparation LeFors had removed the door, planed off the bottom two inches, and rehung it. Behind the gimmicked door, Deputy Sheriff Leslie Snow and district court stenographer Charles Ornhaus were eavesdropping. As soon as LeFors and Horn went downstairs for another drink, Ornhaus, who had taken down the entire interview in shorthand, hurried out to have his notes typed up. A warrant was issued the next morning, and Horn was arrested by the sheriff, a deputy, and Sandy McKneal in the lobby of the Inter-Ocean Hotel, while Joe LeFors looked on.

The trial of Tom Horn for the murder of Willie Nickell was held in the fall of 1902, before a jury of eight ranchers, a cowhand, a butcher, a blacksmith, and a hotel bellhop.

The head of Horn's defense team, engaged on his behalf by Horn's cattle-baron employers, was John W. Lacy, general counsel for the Union Pacific Railroad and former state Supreme Court chief justice. The wealthy stockgrowers were anxious to help Horn in every possible way, because he had the power to implicate some of them as accessories to several—and perhaps dozens—of murders.

Parts of the prosecution's argument were trivial: Horn's admission that he had been riding in the vicinity of the Nickell ranch the day before Willie was shot; the introduction of the record of a court hearing from eleven years earlier, in which Kels Nickell was accused but never formally charged with attacking John Coble, Horn's friend and employer, with a pocket knife. The weight of the state's case rested solely upon the damning, if possibly tainted, confession. Ornhaus's transcript was admitted as evidence, and Joe LeFors attested to its accuracy and the circumstances under which it had been obtained. Both men, and witness Leslie Snow, declared that Horn had been sober throughout the conversation.

Attorney Lacy offered parallel defenses. First, Horn claimed he was intoxicated and bragging during the LeFors interview, and introduced character witnesses to testify that he was a surly, loud-mouthed, blustering drunk. In the alternative, Horn insisted that he had been speaking hypothetically, and only to impress a future employer with his familiarity with the accepted methods of combatting rustlers. According to Horn, portions of the transcript that would support this contention were edited out.

On October 23 Tom Horn was adjudged guilty and condemned to death; on appeal the state Supreme Court sustained the conviction and sentence. But with the verdict, the suspense over the Tom Horn case only tautened. Would Tom Horn "peach" on his employers to save his skin? Would those who sided with him—or those who feared what he knew—try to break him out, or even assassinate him?

The answer to the first question was no. As one Wyoming cattleman said after Horn was finally hanged, "He died without 'squealing,' to the great relief of many very respectable citizens of the West." But during the year between trial and execution, the atmosphere in Cheyenne was a combination of siege and circus.

Before Thanksgiving 1902, it was widely broadcast that Butch Cassidy and the dreaded Wild Bunch were gathering to ride to Tom Horn's liberation. The fact that Butch and Sundance were in Bolivia and that at least half a dozen of the old gang were doing time or dead did little to ruin this tall tale's barroom currency. Meanwhile, Horn occupied his spare moments with escape attempts. He wrote to other prisoners in match-soot on scraps of blanket and shirttail, plotting elaborate liberation schemes. At various times he tried to fashion keys from broom-wire, soup bones, a piece of wood, and shards of glass. On one occasion, Under Sheriff Richard Proctor took a case knife from the prisoner; on another, he found a length of lead pipe hidden in Horn's pant leg.

Then, on August 9, Horn and Jim McCloud, who was charged with armed robbery and who was the only other prisoner on the jail's top floor, managed to overpower Proctor. Although Proctor had the keys in his pocket, he insisted the ring was locked in the safe. The prisoners marched Proctor to the strongbox, but instead of the key he removed a revolver which he fired four times, wounding McCloud slightly.

Horn and McCloud raced downstairs, but by now Proctor was ringing the firebell to give the alarm, and a crowd was converging on the jailhouse. McCloud jumped on the sheriff's horse and rode west, but was captured immediately.

Horn ran on foot in the other direction. Hatless and carrying Proctor's sneak-gun, Horn attracted the attention of a shopkeeper named Eldrich, who pulled his own gun from under the counter, stepped outside and shot Horn in the neck, not seriously. When Horn tried to return fire, he discovered he could not work the modern automatic lock safety of Proctor's pistol. Merchant Eldrich disarmed the desperado, and officers arrived in time to keep the mob from beating Horn to death. As a last adventure, it was an ignominious coda to a notorious career.

In the last days before Horn's execution, the Wyoming capital seemed moonstruck. It was persistently rumored that gangs of cowboys were massing outside town, prepared to sack the town, if necessary, to free Tom Horn. Governor Fenimore Chatterton, himself the object of death threats, called out the state militia, and machine gun nests covered the jail. At least twenty-five sheriff's deputies from all over the state stood rifle guard in nearby buildings and at every window of the courthouse. Sheriff Edward Smalley, a grocer appointed to fill an unexpired term a few weeks before Horn's arrest, nervously warned citizens to approach the jail at their own risk, while every arriving train brought more carloads of morbid curiosity seekers.

On the street in front of the jail, Kels Nickell, father of the victim, patrolled with a shotgun, buttonholing passersby like Coleridge's Ancient Mariner to declare his determination to turn Horn into dogmeat should the killer attempt another jailbreak. Inside on the cell-block, a deathwatch detail stared glumly as Horn completed a horsehair riata he'd been hand-weaving for months. As he worked he could hear the crash and thud from the jailhouse courtyard as two hundred-pound sandbags were dropped through the trap over and over again to test the gallows.

The execution, on November 20, 1903, the day before

Horn's forty-third birthday, was anticlimactic, as it must be. On the way across the courtyard, Horn paused to shake the hands of two old rodeo pards, Charlie and Frank Irwin. Charlie asked if Horn had confessed, and Horn answered no. While Horn stood on the scaffolding, the Irwin boys sang the old railroad hymn, "Keep Your Hand upon the Throttle and Your Eye upon the Rail," which, according to an account in the Chicago *Record-Herald*, brought "tears to the eyes of all except Horn himself." Horn's last words, to County Clerk Joseph Cahill as he adjusted Horn's restraining straps, were, "Ain't losing your nerve are you, Joe?" The trap was sprung at 11:08 in the morning, and sixteen minutes later Horn was pronounced dead of a broken neck. The handpicked witnesses congratulated Under Sheriff Proctor on a flawless execution.

In parts of Wyoming today, smart-mouthing about the Tom Horn case remains a fine way to incite barroom violence. A colleague of ours who grew up in the Iron Mountain country, and whose grandfather occasionally hosted Tom Horn when he rode their part of the range, reports that sentiment in that precinct remains nearly unanimously in Horn's favor. Beyond doubt, the confession upon which his conviction depended would be summarily ruled inadmissible in a modern courtroom. In 1977, when *In Wyoming* magazine published a biographical sketch of Kels Nickell by a nephew, Dennie Trimble Nickell, even this admittedly biased writer does not flatly state that Tom Horn murdered his cousin.

Joe LeFors's role in Tom Horn's downfall did not appreciably affect his life or career. He remained with the U.S. Marshal's office until April of 1908, when he went to work for the Wyoming Wool Growers Association. He was based in Wyoming for another dozen years after that, although he makes vague and tantalizing reference in his autobiography to other adventures during this period, including a "hazardous and thrilling" trip up an unnamed river in Central America; the shipwreck of a native schooner in the Caribbean, "the closest call I ever had;" and travel in Mexico and Argentina "as an officer and also as a private citizen." He moved to southern California in 1921, but returned to Wyoming after a couple of seasons. He was seventy-five when he died on October 1, 1940, in Buffalo, the town where he had settled at the end of the cattle drive that had first brought him to Wyoming fifty-five years earlier.

Joe LeFors was a cop, private or public, for over thirty years, during a period when law was scarcer and gunplay more common than today. He appears to have done a good job. But LeFors lacked the flair for publicity of a Wyatt Earp, the glib good fellowship of a Bat Masterson, or the tragic flaws of a Wild Bill Hickok. The facts of his most noteworthy moment will always be overshadowed by the legend of his adversary, and Joe LeFors will remain a footnote to the last chapter of Western history.

On the day he died, Tom Horn gave John Coble a penciled manuscript, which Coble published the next year as *Life of Tom Horn by Himself*. It is a vividly written description of Horn's days as an Indian fighter and Pinkerton, but it ends with Horn's arrival in Wyoming in 1894. *I, Tom Horn*, a superb novel by Will Henry, takes as its conceit the discovery in 1973 of a second Horn autobiography in which Horn tells the rest of the story and stoutly denies his guilt in the Nickell killing. In Henry's version, the transcript of the confession was edited by LeFors to delete Horn's denial of his guilt.

In his biography, *The Saga of Tom Horn*, Dean Krakel

also argues that Horn was innocent of the Nickell killing, although Krakel acknowledges that Horn was a hired killer for cattle interests. Another excellent Horn biography is *The Last of the Badmen*, by Jay Monaghan. A detailed treatment of Horn's career as a hired gun appears in *The Gunfighters* volume of the Time/Life series, *The Old West*. For reproductions of several contemporary newspaper accounts of the Tom Horn affair, as well as photographs of the principals, see *The Authentic Wild West: The Gunfighters*, by James D. Horan.

Joe LeFors wrote his autobiography, *Wyoming Peace Officer*, shortly before his death, but it was not published until 1953. LeFors was also the prototype of the title character of *Whispering Smith*, a best-selling novel by Frank H. Spearman (1859–1937) that was filmed in silent and sound versions; in the latter (1948, directed by Leslie Fenton), Alan Ladd plays Spearman's soft-spoken special agent. In the movie *Butch Cassidy and the Sundance Kid* (1969, George Roy Hill), Joe LeFors is the leader of the posse that bursts out of an Overland Flyer boxcar and gives chase after the gang stops the Union Pacific train for the second time. Then there is *Tom Horn* (1980, William Wiard), starring Steve McQueen in his penultimate film before his death. The rest of the casting is equally good, the photography gorgeous, but the script and direction turns the story of the last gunfighter into ninety-eight minutes of tedium; the film was almost withheld from release altogether.

William Kittredge
Steven M. Krauzer
Missoula, Montana
Summer 1984

About the Authors

Owen Rountree is the pseudonym of Steven M. Krauzer and William Kittredge, who live in Missoula, Montana. Kittredge, Professor of English at the University of Montana, has published two collections of short stories, most recently *We Are Not In This Together*, edited by Raymond Carver (Graywolf Press, Port Townsend, Washington). As Adam Lassiter, Krauzer is the author of the *Dennison's War* series of action thrillers. In addition to their collaboration as Owen Rountree, Kittredge and Krauzer have edited four anthologies of popular American fiction under their own names.

GREAT TALES from the OLD WEST

OWEN ROUNTREE